JASON STEED

Absolutely Nothing

Book 3 in the Jason Steed Series.

Mark A. Cooper

www.markacooper.com

ISBN:1492259683
ISBN-13: 978-1492259688

I ask children to forgive me for dedicating this book to a grown-up. I have a real excuse; this grown-up is the best friend I have in the world. Dedicated to my beautiful loving wife

Without her, none of this would be possible.

Sandra,

I thank you and will always love you.

Cover artwork by **Tadas Sidlauskas**

Prelude

On April 4, 1975, fourteen-year-old Abigail Giles left Manchester's Town Hill High School at lunchtime. She caught a bus to Manchester's train station and boarded a train bound for Paddington Station, London. She wore just her school uniform and had a backpack with a change of clothes and her lunch money.

Her adolescent mind was filled with rage after an argument with her parents. *I'll show them. They'll be sorry,* she told herself, oblivious to the dangers she faced as she ran away and headed to the bright lights of London.

Chapter One

Jason threw his school backpack across the polished wooden floor and slammed the front door shut behind him. The bang echoed around the large entrance hall. As his backpack smashed into the foot of the stairs, he kicked off his shoes and stomped up to his bedroom, removing his school tie and leaving a trail of clothing scattered behind himself.

His father, Raymond Steed, watched his son from his office and slowly followed Jason to his room, picking up after him. Ray knocked at his door and waited.

"What?" snapped Jason aggressively. He had stripped off his school uniform and was putting on his tracksuit.

"Can I come in?" Ray asked through the door.

"Yes" Jason sighed.

Ray entered and looked at him. He carried Jason's school backpack, tie, and shoes.

“What happened?”

“I hate that school. Why can’t I go to a sports school that doesn’t force you to do science and religious studies?” He groaned as he pulled on his training shoes.

“Do I have to ask again?” his father asked, raising his eyebrows. He looked into his sons sapphire blue eyes. Most of the time Jason's blond hair fell over them and hid where he was looking. Ray had given up years ago trying to get his son to have his fringe cut to a normal length. Jason always preferred having it over his eyes.

“I came bottom in History and Religious Education. And according to Mr. Griffiths I’m ‘below average’ in Math,” Jason said putting on a posh upper crust accent. “He never said anything about me coming top in German, French, and Spanish language. He'll be writing to you and has given me enough homework to last ten years. I’m gonna die of nerdism.”

“*Nerdism?* Is that a word?” His father smiled affectionately.

“It is now.” Jason frowned, trying to conceal a smirk. “So I was bottom in two subjects. I’m top in three others. I hate that stupid Welsh Headmaster.”

“So where do you think you’re going?”

“It’s Tuesday, I’ve got Karate.”

“Not until this has been done,” Ray said,

holding out Jason's backpack.

“Dad. You know I go karate on Tuesdays. I can’t stop that. I'd end up a nerd,” Jason whined.

“No, you will end up a ‘drop out’ if you don’t get your grades up. Don’t expect to be able to join the Marines or S.A.S if you fail all your exams.”

“Okay, I’ll start it when I get back.”

“No. You will start it now. You may have to cut out either karate from twice a week to once a week or cut out Sea Cadets or Judo. Weekends, you can’t see Catherine or Scott unless you have completed *all* your homework.”

“I always do *all* my homework. I’m just not very good at it. We can’t all be a brain box like Scott.” Jason sat heavily on his bed in a sulk.

“I’ll let you go tonight, but when you get back I want you to do your homework. If you need help, just ask. Together we can improve your grades.”

“It's just *so* boring. What use is it to me knowing about King Henry VIII? Do you know all the names of his six wives?” Jason asked, hoping to prove his point.

Ray paused and smiled. “Catherine of Aragon, Anne Boleyn, Jane Seymour, Katherine Howard, and Catherine Parr. I can’t think of the other one or what order.”

Oh wow, my dad is a nerd, Jason thought to

himself.

"What does that prove?" Jason sighed.

"Not much, as I don't need to know that, but it's all part of learning and growing up. *Got it!* The other wife was Anne of Cleaves." Ray grinned.

It's official. My Dad's a nerd.

"Okay, okay. I'*ll* do it when I get back, but it still seems pointless to me."

*

Even with his father's help, Jason continued to struggle with some aspects at school. He was exceptional in foreign languages and, although he was one of the greatest martial arts experts in the country, no grades were given for that. St. Joseph's Boys School was one of the top private schools in Great Britain and had some of the brightest pupils. His best friend Scott Turner had an IQ of 168. Only a handful of people in the country could better that. When Jason's books were marked alongside Scott's it didn't help matters.

*

Jason picked at his food in the school Canteen. He and Scott sat together eating. He had been training harder than normal. Around Christmas he'd begun studying another form of karate, Jeet Kune Do. He already held three black belts in Karate, one was a 3rd Dan, plus he held a black belt in Judo. His hero Bruce Lee created Jeet

Kune Do and therefore he wanted to master it.

Last night he had been sparing with a grand master and 3rd Dan black belt at Jeet Kune Do. Jason had lost concentration and was kicked in the chest. He suspected he might have cracked a rib. Breathing heavily caused a pain across his chest.

"You seem quiet today Jase, everything okay?" Scott asked, stealing one of Jason's uneaten sausages. Scott was the same age as Jason, with brown hair and large brown eyes. The two boys were very close.

"Yeah, I got hurt at karate last night, just not feeling myself today," Jason replied.

"I'd rather not know about you feeling yourself Jase, not while I'm eating a sausage," Scott joked, making a rude gesture as he ate. Jason smiled at the remark and felt his chest. He would normally laugh at Scott's jokes but wasn't feeling up to it today, despite Scott's attempts to lift his spirits.

When school was over they walked home together, discussing music and the latest Jackson Five song.

"I got hairs now." Scott grinned.

"What?" Jason asked.

"Well, three to be precise." Scott smiled proudly pointing down to his nether regions.

"And you're telling me this, *why*?" Jason asked annoyed. He flicked his blond bangs across his face and glared at Scott.

"Don't be such a grumpy guts all day. So you got hurt at karate get over it. I thought we were friends and was just talking. If I can't tell my best friend something as important as that who can I tell?" Scott snapped back and started to walk ahead.

Jason let him go a few paces and finally ran and caught up. "I don't have any there yet, but I got two under my right arm pit growing." Jason grinned.

"You're blond and fair skinned, so you may be a bit slower than me. Our voices should break this year. Russell Jennings' voice has already broken," Scott said, trying to put on a deep voice.

"Can you help me with math homework tonight? I have no idea how that algebra stuff works."

"*Jase*. Mr. Thomas asked if everybody understood it. Why didn't you say anything?" Scott frowned.

"I didn't want to look any more stupid than I do now. I can't see the point of X equals Y. What good is that? It's bad enough with basic stuff."

"Yes I'll show you, it's important and fun." Scott paused thinking, of a use for Jason.

Jason fought against calling Scott a nerd. He knew he hated being called that, and now was not the time to upset him, especially if he needed Scotts help with his homework.

"Okay, lets think about you flying a plane. I mean a big jet aircraft. The actual math used in the cockpit is basic addition and subtraction for a weight and balance manifest and basic algebra with rounded numbers to figure descents in your head."

Nerd. Jason struggled to keep his thoughts to himself. "Okay you made your point. When we get to my place just show me slowly how you get the bloody numbers to equal letters. You can stay for dinner."

The twelve-year-old boys lay on the rug in Jason's room going over the homework. When Ray entered, both boys ignored him and continued working. Their school shoes, jackets, and ties lay in a heap on the floor. Ray smiled as he watched Scott explain algebra to Jason. He put it in a language Jason could follow so he soon grasped the concept.

"Sorry to interrupt boys. Jason, Captain Bill Giles, his brother, and sister-in-law are coming tonight to stay for a few days," Ray said.

"What, Bill Giles from HMS Stoke?" Jason asked without turning around.

"Yes. His niece has gone missing. Her friends told them she left Manchester and jumped on the train to London."

Jason turned around and lifted himself onto one elbow, looking up at his father. "As long as he doesn't expect me to salute him when I'm in my Sea Cadet uniform, not in my own home. Although it will be nice to see him again."

Two hours later Ray walked up the stairs to collect Scott and take him home. The boys were playing a new record Scott had leant Jason. It was by a group called 'Hot Butter' the fast instrumental electronic tune was rightly named 'Popcorn.'

Because of the volume, they never heard him knock so Ray walked in. Both boys were stripped to the waist dancing in sequence to the tune. Stepping forward two steps and back one before shifting to the left along with the music, they danced faster as the tune increased in speed.

The sight amused Ray. Once it finished, both Scott and Jason turned to see they had an audience. Scott's face was flushed. Ray wasn't sure if it was embarrassment or exhaustion from dancing so fast. He gave a small applause until he noticed the dirty look he got from Jason.

*

Jason returned home from school in better spirits the following day. Thanks to Scott's help he had grasped algebra and two of the afternoon subjects were foreign languages, something he enjoyed and excelled in. Jason trotted down the grand staircase in his Sea Cadet uniform and noticed a man and woman enter the front door. He continued down and adjusted his uniform. They both looked up at Jason and smiled.

"You must be Jason." The woman smiled. She looked right through Jason as if her mind was elsewhere.

"Yeah, hi. You must be Bill Giles's sister-in-law," Jason said as he held out his hand. Her eyes were blood shot. Jason thought she looked as if she had been crying.

"Yes sweetheart, I'm Pauline. This is Ian." She bent down and took off her shoes.

"Hi, Jason. It's nice to finally meet you. You were in bed last night when we arrived and had gone to school this morning before we got up. Are you going out again?" Ian asked.

Jason looked at him. He was a younger version of his brother Bill. "Yeah I've got Sea Cadets tonight." Jason Paused. Bill walked in, followed by Jason's father. Bill smiled gave a nod and saluted. Jason, out of habit, saluted back.

You Dodo. Why'd you salute back? Jason chastised himself. It made it worse when he caught his father grinning at him. Jason gave his father a '*Don't say a word look'* and shook Bill's hand.

"Jason do you want to give Cadets a miss tonight and come out to dinner with us? We could do with cheering up," Ray asked.

"I had dinner already with Mrs. Beeton. Thanks though," Jason replied, giving his father a welcome hug. He pulled away after picking up on his father's stiffness as he turned down the offer. "How did it go today?" Jason asked, trying to sound interested.

"Bloody terrible. You got any Port in the

house? I could do with a stiff drink before dinner. I can't believe how incompetent the Metropolitan Police are," Bill interrupted angrily.

"Why, what happened with them? They're normally helpful."

Ray paced to the liquor cabinet in living room and opened a bottle of port and poured four glasses while Bill explained everything to Jason.

"You wouldn't believe how many teenagers run away from home to the bright lights of London. Over seventy-five thousand a year according to the police. Apparently some turn up at the Salvation Army after a night or two out in the cold. They basically told us to go home and wait. Abigail has been missing for four days. We can't just go back to Manchester and sit around and wait," Bill said. He drank his glass of Port in one swallow, then helped himself to another and started to pace up and down.

"My sister is staying at our home just in case Abigail calls home. I'm not leaving London without her." Pauline sobbed. Ian put his arm around her and comforted her. An awkward silence engulfed the room.

Eventually Jason broke the silence. "I know people at Scotland Yard. Well, actually Scotland Yard Undercover Intel. They owe me a favour. I can call and ask if they can help." He smiled, took off his cap, and plucked his blond fringe of hair down in front of his eyes.

Six months had passed since Jason had gone

undercover for SYUI and Inspector George Young. He'd helped uncover a drug smuggling plot with the Triad. George Young was now head of SYUI.

Despite many attempts by George to use Jason again to work undercover, Ray wouldn't allow it. He'd actually banned George from having any contact with Jason again.

Jason looked at his father before he dialled SYUI. Ray reluctantly nodded and gave him the go ahead to make the call. The phone was picked up on the second ring. Jason asked the phone operator at SYUI to speak to George Young. The operator sighed when she heard a child's voice and took Jason's name while placing him on hold after telling him Mr Young is a very busy man. She seemed surprised when she came back on the line, saying George instantly agreed to speak to Jason.

"Jason Steed. Is it really you?" George asked.

"Yeah, hi George." Jason grinned.

"Does your old man know you're calling me?"

"Yes, Dad's here with me. I need to ask a favour, George."

"Anything to help you, Jason. What can I do?"

"Can we come in and see you?" Jason asked.

"*We*? Sure come on in. I'll be here for a couple more hours."

*

Jason, his father, and the Giles family waited at the reception desk while the desk sergeant sent a message to SYUI. When George appeared he headed for Jason and held out his hand. Jason ignored the hand and gave George a hug instead, much to the surprise of the others.

George was dressed in his usual attire—black pants, white shirt, and a black jacket with matching tie. As usual, he smelt of cigarettes and body odour and his hair was greasy. Jason thought he looked just as unhealthy as he always did. His stomach over hung his pants and his shirt buttons were straining at the seams.

George and Ray shook hands; there was no love between them, but they made an effort for Jason's sake. Ray introduced Bill and Ian, but George moved directly to Pauline. He took her hand, sat down with her, and looked up at Jason waiting for an explanation. The man had a knack for knowing when someone was in trouble.

"Pauline's daughter Abigail ran away from home. She's only fourteen, but her friend said Abigail was heading here from Manchester," Jason said giving a tight-lipped smile. He studied George and thought the man looked a bit fatter than he remembered.

"Do we know why she ran away?" George asked, stroking Pauline's hand.

She was unable to answer and started to cry,

so Ian explained. “Abigail went ahead and got her tongue pierced after we told her not to do it. We had a huge argument about it. She never came home from school and told her friend she was going to London. She has this dream and wants to be an actress one day.” Ian held Pauline’s other hand while he spoke.

“Okay, come with me.” George sighed before he put his hand over his mouth while he loudly burped. He walked ahead down a long corridor. The corridor was line with large offices, each with glass doors. George paused and spun around. “Look, we don’t normally allow members of the public in here, but since you’re with Jason and he works for us, I’ll make an exception. Some of this is classified, so forget what you see once you leave.”

Ray frowned at George’s remark.

George stopped at the first door and looked in. Inside, two officers were going through papers in manila files. Another was talking on a phone. On the walls were pictures of men, some taken without their knowledge from a distance.

“This is our criminal underworld dept.” George said opening the door.

The officers looked up and nodded as the guests walked in. George pointed at a board with a picture of a large man with white hair and a broken boxer’s nose.

"This is Mick Vango. I’ve been after this geezer for years. Because of the intimidation of jurors, he got away with murder after he killed a nightclub owner. He's known as 'The Hammer.' hen he was younger he was a boxer. He was also the best man at Robbie Kemp's wedding. You know Robbie Kemp from the notorious 'Kemp Twins.' We know he's still stealing everything that's not tied down and now has moved onto dodgy cars and drugs. It's just a matter of time before I get him behind bars."

George passed the next few offices without mentioning what cases they were investigating. He paused at an office and looked down at Jason.

"This is where we keep track of your old friends Jason, the Triad." George winked. Jason looked through the glass window but kept walking. "It's quiet in there now thanks to you. We just check on their activities to see if we can sniff out anything."

Jason shuddered as he thought about his last mission. It was something he wanted to put behind him. He went undercover in a boy's detention center to befriend a Triad leader's son. Although the mission was a success, it had almost cost Jason his life.

"Ah here we are." George sighed loudly as he opened a door to an office. They followed him and gasped at the sight of the wall of photographs of children, mostly aged between eleven and sixteen. Most of the pictures were school photographs and showed the children in uniforms a variety of colors and styles from around Great Britain.

"Are all these children missing?" Ray asked

astonished, glancing over the fresh young faces.

"Sadly, this is just the ones who have turned up dead. There are thousands of kids who run away and come to London. Unfortunately, maybe two to three hundred turn up dead each year," George said casually. "Across the UK, over seventy thousand kids aged eleven to sixteen run away from home every year. They travel across the country and arrive here in London, mostly via the train from their hometown or city connecting stations. Beneath the attraction of London's bright lights and historic city hides a much darker side. A seedy underground network that prey on these young runaways.

Thousands never return home. Some are forced to work for no money. The lucky ones get menial jobs in sweat factories. Unlucky ones just roam the streets. Some are locked up in youth detention centers for theft. The remainder are never seen again. We believe they're sold on an international black market for body parts or forced into illegal activities, becoming entangled in our gruesome underworld."

Pauline and Ian looked horrified. Pauline started to cry.

"I'm not saying your daughter's dead, far from it. If I can help in anyway then these people can." George said pointing at two male officers and a stern looking lady officer. George explained to his officers the situation. They glanced over at Jason and started to speak among themselves. The woman officer came over and shook Jason's hand.

"So you're the famous Jason Steed. It's nice to meet you at last. I was a junior detective when you were working for us on the Boudica Triad case. I work here in the illegal children's labor dept no. I'm Barbara Inkpen. Please, call me Barb." She smiled.

George interrupted and explained that London had over twenty gangs that he knew of that worked selling children. It was cold hearing the real life events that happened in the back streets of London. Children as young as eleven were sold like animals to rich clients, and some were used for organ transplants. Healthy young organs could fetch a fortune. Many of the donors would be left in unsanitary conditions and die in agony.

George was optimistic that Abigail was probably just roaming the streets with other young runaways she had met up with. He just wanted them to be prepared for the worst.

"She would have arrived at Paddington train station," Bill explained in his upper class accent. "Surely one has people watching the station?"

"Paddington has over two hundred thousand people a day passing through. Maybe twenty-five to thirty thousand are school age children, either going to school or visiting family. Do you propose we stop and interrogate every child under sixteen? Not to mention they likely wouldn't tell the truth," George snapped.

"Then what did you bring us in here for?" Bill asked anxiously. "How on earth is this helping?"

"Well," George said loudly. He looked at Jason and gave a smile. "If we could have a kid run away, get a train to Paddington, and hang out and see who attempts to pick them up we may have a lead. It would of course be safe. We'd keep watch from a distance. But the kid would have to be able to look after himself if there was a problem."

"No way." Ray snorted. "George Young, you never bloody give up do you? Jason has done more for his country than anyone should have to do. How can you even think of using him again?"

George sat on the end of a desk and folded his arms with a straight face. "Unless you've got another idea how to get on the inside and find out where these kids get taken, then I guess you lot had better start walking the streets of London looking. But if there is anyone who could do this, Jason could. If they picked up Jason it would be like handing them a ticking bomb. If they tried to touch him, he would rip 'em apart."

"It would work. He's extremely good looking, small and blond. Many would pay a high price for someone like him." Brenda smiled at Jason who was blushing. "I love how you have your blond hair hanging over your eyes, you look so cute."

Chapter Two

Reluctantly, Ray Steed agreed to allow Jason to work as a decoy for the undercover operation. Jason was delighted to get time off school and to work for SYUI again.

He also insisted his best friend Scott worked at SYUI while he was undercover. Jason trusted Scott; he had twice before been an advantage. Scott would help monitor his progress. If Jason needed to meet with someone to pass information, it would look harmless if he was just talking to another boy his own age.

While preparing to go undercover Jason and Scott spent a day reading some of the case files from the missing or dead children. Jason was physically sick when he read some of the files and learned what some children were forced to do. It made him more determined to work undercover and try to help save some of the runaways.

Raymond Steed drove Jason fifty miles out of London to Reading train Station. Reading was a major bypass station most travellers would pass through. It made sense to board here. Scott went along for the car ride to keep Jason Company.

SYUI were already in place at Paddington train station; one of the officers was working at the newsstand. It was a busy Sunday and he was angry at the amount of newspapers he was forced to sell to members of the public. Cursing under his breath that he did not join the police force to sell newspapers. Other officers were in similar positions; one was emptying trashcans and picking up trash, while a few others acted as passengers roaming around as if waiting for a train.

*

Jason took a deep breath of fresh air as they climbed out of the car. Scott stretched his arms and yawned.

"Jase, why are railroads always angry?" Scott grinned.

Jason hated to ask he knew Scott was going to throw a hundred jokes at him. "I dunno. Why are railroads angry?" Jason asked.

"Because people keep crossing them." He laughed and Jason grinned once outside the station, he gave his dad a hug and a kiss goodbye.

"I'll be home in a couple of days at the most, Dad. Don't worry." Jason said.

"But I will worry. Look after yourself. As soon as someone tries to pick you up, let SYUI take over," Ray said, holding Jason so tight he could hardly breathe. They kissed again. Jason gave Scott a quick 'man hug' goodbye.

"See ya, mate. It'll be nice to miss school tomorrow." Jason laughed.

"Yeah, I'm going straight to SYUI. As soon as you know something call in. Oh here you *must* take this," Scott said passing Jason some gum.

"Thanks why *must* I?" he asked surprised.

"'This is so you can do what a train does—chew, chew, Choo." Scott grinned.

Jason found himself in a half full carriage with mostly adults reading newspapers. For the most part of the journey he sat alone and looked out the window as the scenery flashed by. He checked his pockets; he had some money, change for a phone call, a small pocketknife, and the gum Scott gave him. He had a backpack with some clean underwear, socks, shirt, toothbrush, and comb.

Once he stepped off the train at Paddington, a strange feeling came over him. Jason could never describe it. The blood in his body pumped harder and hotter. It was how he felt when he was left alone on Jakarta after the massacre. He was alone, yet found an inner strength. It made him alert and able to focus and absorb his surroundings, pulling and funnelling information in into his brain.

He zipped up the front of his jacket and slowly walked along the platform until he was through the ticket gate with the other passengers.

Paddington station was a massive building. He looked up at the ceiling in awe. Huge steel rafters covered with pigeons supported the roof; each rafter had a series of star shapes cut out. Jason wondered why. The station had various shops, kiosks, and cafés.

He noticed a newsstand, and he studied the man working. They gave each other a paused glance before Jason continued walking. He spent six hours wandering around the shops. He bought himself a coke with a five-pound note his father gave him. He never noticed a black youth watching him as he stuffed the change back in his pocket.

Jason knew George Young had planted several agents around the station and would be here himself somewhere. To help pass the time he tried to work out who was working for SYUI and who was just a member of public or actually worked for British Rail.

After drinking his coke, he made his way to the men's bathroom and started to relieve himself. He looked at the chrome water pipe in front that flushed the urinal and watched his reflection. He noticed the black youth come in behind him. As if he had a sixth sense he could feel the boy watching him and watching the door. Jason turned his head for second to look at him. He thought the boy looked about fifteen, wearing dirty jeans and a Millwall Football Club black hoodie.

Jason looked back to the front. From the chrome pipe he could see the youth take out what looked like a knife from his back pocket. He hadn't time to finish, but he stopped and dribbled down his leg as he tucked himself away and did up his zipper.

Jason turned.

"Hand over the money and I may not cut up your pretty face," the youth said, waving the knife towards Jason.

Jason span on one leg and threw a roundhouse kick. It hit the soft target in the youth's stomach, knocking the wind out of him. The boy was thrown back against the sinks and fell forward gasping for air. Jason kicked out again twice in rapid succession to the face. The youth's head was knocked back against the sink, cut open and oozing blood. He slid down, leaving a blood stained smear down the tiled wall. He was out cold.

"I like my face the way it is thanks." Jason cursed at him. He approached and pulled his leg back to kick him again, but stopped short. The youth wasn't moving, Jason thought that he may have over reacted and was now concerned he may have seriously hurt him. Plus he looked even younger now he was lying motionless. He ran outside to the man on the newsstand.

"I think I may have hurt someone in the bathroom, he was a mugger he tried to rob me," Jason said sheepishly.

The undercover officer looked around to make sure no one was watching.

"Go away; I'll take care of it," he whispered. He ducked down behind the counter and contacted the SYUI unit on his radio.

Jason strolled back to the center of the station and sat on a bench, not knowing if he had spoilt the mission. He watched two men in suits enter the bathroom. Five minutes later an ambulance crew went in with a stretcher. Jason watched from a distance as they carried the youth out.

A small crowd gathered to watch. One of the men was talking to George Young who seemed to have appeared out of thin air. They all watched the boy get carried away in the ambulance with its lights flashing.

George paced directly towards Jason. It was obvious he was angry. His eyes looked like they were going to explode as he glared at Jason.

I'm in for it now, Jason thought to himself, sure he had blown the whole operation and wasted everyone's time. He knew he wasn't allowed to use martial arts on members of the public. He should have just left. Even in self-defence he was legally supposed to verbally warn the person that he has martial arts skills. Now the whole operation could be off because he'd lost his temper. Worse still, if the youth was severely injured or worse, Jason could be in serious trouble.

George immediately verbally attacked Jason. It started with "What the hell is wrong with you?" He continued to rant and rave for nearly four minutes, going over and over how much the manpower had cost to set up the mission and how Jason's quick temper had ruined it before it started and put an teenager in hospital. Eventually, George took a breath and asked Jason what he had to say for himself.

Jason sheepishly looked up. Some of the commuters watched. They didn't know what was happening, but they could clearly see a young boy being shouted at. To look at the pair of them, you could have mistaken it for father scolding his son.

"George, I'm sorry. But that's why they put easers on pencils. We all make mistakes, and that guy had a knife and wanted my money. Suppose I was a normal boy in there without martial art skills," Jason said. He stood up to face George.

"And just how are you going to help Abigail now? There are another hundred teenage thugs like that in London. Half killing them won't clear up the problem." George spat.

"What do we do now?" Barbara Inkpen asked. She joined in, giving the reprimanding glare to Jason.

"Pack up and let's go home, but first go to the hospital and see what happened to the mugger. I'm sure he won't make a complaint, and he has no idea Jason was working for us, so it may just go away," George said. He turned, giving Jason a final glare before storming off.

"What about me?" Jason meekly asked.

George turned and shouted back so loud it even made Barbara jump.

"*Go home!* And get some help with that bloody temper of yours. That's the third time you've nearly killed someone unnecessarily."

Jason stood quietly. Deep down, he knew he had gone too far in certain cases, but it was always a case of self-defence. His problem was he couldn't stop himself once he was pumped up with adrenaline in a fight. Nevertheless, he was visibly shaken by the verbal reprimand from George, someone he'd considered a friend. He sat back down on the bench and twiddled his fingers, biting his bottom lip.

"Come on. I'll give you a lift home Jason." Barbara smiled, holding out her hand. Jason looked up at her.

He wasn't a baby that needed his hand held he told himself. "I'll catch a taxi. I wouldn't want to waste more of SYUI's money," Jason snapped.

"Are you sure?" she asked.

"Yes. Just go". He watched under his blond bangs as the undercover team started to leave. A woman had sat reading gave him a dirty look as she stood and left.

"You mean I spent five hours picking up trash for nothing?" a man's angry voice said as Barbara told him the operation was called off. Jason thought he was a janitor who was sweeping the station floor. The undercover officer looked at Jason and shook his head from side to side.

Jason took a deep breath. He felt like everyone in the station was glaring at him. He slowly walked outside of the station, stopping and watching some passengers saying goodbye to family as they caught a train. He dug in his pocket and realized he never had enough money for a taxi. He thought about a bus, but wasn't certain which bus would be going in his direction. When he had been in London in the past on buses, he was either with Scott, who could memorize all the bus routes, or he had known what number buses to catch. Reluctantly, he walked back inside the station to find Barbara.

After five minutes of searching he gave up. The entire SYUI team had packed up and left. He felt pretty stupid for turning down the ride home, so he made his way to the large bus timetable on the wall. He examined it until he found some familiar places, made a mental note of the bus numbers, and walked up onto the street looking for the bus stop with the relevant numbers. Once he found the bus stop he sat on a bench waiting.

Chapter Three

A boy about fourteen came out of nowhere and sat next to Jason on the bench.

"Got any cigs on yer?" the boy asked in a broad cockney accent.

"No, I don't smoke," Jason replied, looking at the youth. He was taller than Jason, stocky built, with short brown hair. He was wearing a black leather jacket, blue jeans, and 'Doc Martin' black boots. Jason thought he looked dirty.

"Got any money?" he asked, now sitting on the back of the bench with his feet on the seat.

"That's my business."

"You gotta big mouth for a small kid. How old are you?" he asked, looking down at Jason.

I'm not in the mood for a fight, but if you want to start that's fine with me, Jason said to himself.

"Twelve."

"I've been watching yer. Lost are yer?" he asked, taking out some gum from his pocket.

"No. I know where I am."

"So what you doing here then mate?"

Jason paused. He knew the mission was off now, but thought he would play along; this could be the contact he had previously wanted.

"I run away from home," Jason said proudly.

"Oh, you're a big boy now then. *So* big boy, I spose you got a nice comfy bed to sleep in tonight have yer? Maybe some money for hot food?"

Jason pulled out his money, purposely letting the youth see it.

"I got enough for fish & chips."

"If you hang around here, the 'Old Bill' will pick you up. You can't sleep on the station. They'll send you back to your mommy."

"Then I won't stay here. I'll go into London."

"You're in bloody London. You're a right green one you are." He laughed and passed a piece of gum to Jason. A young woman aged around eighteen drew his and Jason's attention. She wore a short skirt and tight fitting top. She briskly walked past, struggling to walk in her high heel shoes.

'Old Bill' is London cockney slang for Police.

"She's called 'Butter face,'" the boy said.

"Butter face? Do you know her?" Jason asked, taking the gum.

"No but that's what we call a bird like that. She's got a good body, nice legs, and all that good stuff, if ya know what I mean. Everything, *but her face.* " He grinned. Jason roared with laughter. The youth slid down the back of the bench and held out his hand.

"I'm Ricky Ramon, you can call me Ricky."

"I'm Jason Norris." Jason grinned. He had chosen the name Norris after one of his idols, Chuck Norris, the current world karate champion.

"Okay Jason, I'll tell yer what. You get the fish and chips, and you can sleep at my gaff. But first you gotta tell me why you ran from home," Ricky said.

"My parents split, got new partners now, and they both have got young kids. I've been in a bit of trouble, bunking off school, shoplifting, and smashing windows." Jason forced a laugh. "I even lit a huge bonfire that was made for a fireworks display." This was something Jason read on a case file.

"What was wrong with that?" Ricky asked.

"I set light to it a day early." Jason grinned.

"Nice one." He got up and zipped up his jacket. "Come on, let's get some tucker. It's getting late, and the Old Bill will be around soon."

Jason followed Ricky towards the exit. He was unsure if Ricky was part of any gang or just a teenager looking for friends, but it was a start. Maybe he didn't need SYUI back up he told himself. He would find Abigail himself or at least he would try. It would be better than going home and telling the Giles family that he blew it.

After eating the newspaper wrapped fish and chips, Ricky took Jason back down to Paddington Station. They walked down two flights of steps to the underground subway station. Ricky jumped over the turnstile that you really needed a ticket to get through. Jason jumped over and followed. A platform guard shouted for them to come back, but Ricky took to his heels and, with Jason behind him, they ran down two flights of stairs. The cold subway air gave them a new lease of energy; they both roared with laughter as they entered the platform. Jason would never admit it, but he enjoyed being a rebel for a few moments.

A rush of cold air coming from the black tunnel told them a train was coming. It was fairly empty. Ricky climbed on with Jason behind, then they say down together grinning.

"I never buy a ticket." Ricky grinned.

"What, never?" Jason asked.

"Nope. If I went to school I would get a travel

pass, so I figure I should go free anyway." He sat back and folded his hands behind his head.

"Don't you go to school?" Jason asked, copying Ricky and placing his own hands behind his head.

"You're having a laugh aren't you? Me? School? Not bloody likely, mate. I get plenty of money. I don't need school." Ricky took out a bundle of pound notes.

"Wow, what do you do to earn that?"

"Can't say, but maybe I could get you a job there, if you're interested that is?"

"Course. I just spent the last of my money," Jason said. He was now starting to feel he may have gotten lucky, and Ricky could lead him somewhere.

They passed several stations before getting off at Embankment Station and then boarding another train and eventually getting off at Charring Cross. As they walked up Greek Street towards Soho, the reality hit Jason. This was not the best place to be at night.

A drunk crouched in a corner throwing up. Across the street, two women were screaming at each other over one of the woman's ex-boyfriend. Ricky started walking down a dark alley. Jason paused. His gut reaction was too steer clear of places like this, but if he was to stand any chance of finding Abigail or stopping child trafficking he had to stick with Ricky. He took a deep breath and followed.

A right turn took him onto a concrete ramp misted with steam curling out of a restaurant kitchen window. It was stinking of the trash overflowing from a dumpster. A huge fat rat jumped onto the edge and sniffed the air, its whiskers flicking from side to side. Kitchen staff stood in a doorway smoking and cavorting. Next to the kitchen door was another door. It was stuck, but Ricky pushed it with his shoulder as he twisted the handle.

It opened into a narrow hallway. A blue light from a television escaped from the crack in the curtains. Ricky climbed out a window at the end of the hallway onto a metal stairway outside. He ran up the steps two at a time. Once at the top, he pulled a loose brick from the wall and took out a key and open a dirty brown door, Jason followed him inside.

"It's not Buckingham Palace, but its dry, very cheap, and all mine." Ricky grinned, lighting some candles.

Jason took in his surroundings. It was a small damp room with a bed against the wall. A chrome clothes rail on wheels, the type normally seen in clothing stores, stood next to the bed with some clothes hanging. Jason guessed they were Ricky's clothes due to the size. He had a table and one chair. Against the wall was an old sofa; in the candlelight it was difficult to make out the color. A couple of posters of naked women caught Jason's attention.

A small room exited off from the main room, it contained a sink, a bath, and a toilet that looked like it hadn't been cleaned in years.

"You got no electric?" Jason asked. Ricky looked up. He turned on a battery-powered transistor radio.

"I said it's not Buckingham Palace. I don't need electric. I got water, and it's cold so when I take a bath I'm in and out in two minutes. Sometimes I go to the public swimming pool; its heated and they have hot showers. I only sleep here. It belongs to my boss."

"It's nice I suppose." Jason forced a smile.

Ricky took a blanket off his bed and threw it at Jason.

"You can sleep on the couch; it's plenty long enough for you. Tomorrow, I'll take you to my boss." Ricky kicked off his shoes and pulled his socks off. He gave them a sniff and screwed his face up. He took them to the sink, washed them and hung them over the back of a chair to dry. He stripped off to his underwear before climbing into bed. Jason took off his jacket and shoes, but kept the rest on to keep warm.

*

Ray Steed called SYUI the following morning and asked to speak to Barbara Inkpen.

"Hello, Mr. Steed. How can I help you?" Barbara asked in her usual bubbly tone.

"I know you said you would call me at noon with Jason's progress, but I didn't sleep that well and just wanted to know how it went," Ray asked.

Barbara paused.

"Mr. Steed, why are you asking me?"

"You told me that you would be my liaison with Jason and I could call anytime."

"Jason should be home with you, sir." A terrible feeling started to snake around her insides she was dreading the reply.

"Are you bloody joking or what? Jason is working for you." Ray raised his voice.

"No sir, the mission went wrong, and George called it off. Jason was going to catch a taxi home at about seven last night."

Ray threw some of the best curse words at the SYUI officer he had in his arsenal. And after serving for sixteen years in the Royal Navy he had quite a large vocabulary. He was incensed that they had lost touch with Jason. SYUI immediately put out an alert for Jason

When George heard the news, he wasn't too concerned. He knew if anyone could look after himself, Jason could.

*

"You got any money left?" Ricky asked.

"No." Jason yawned, stretching his arms.

"Well, today will be a first and last. The first and last time I buy you breakfast. Got it?"

"Yeah, thanks. If you get me a job, I won't need your money." Jason smiled.

"So would you do *anything* for money and a place to live?" Ricky asked.

"Anything?" Jason paused. "I suppose, I gotta eat and live somewhere. I'm not going home." He smiled, took out his comb, and tried to get his hair under control. His long, blond bangs were sticking up in all directions. After wetting it, he soon got it to look how he wanted it.

They went to a small café called Mick's. Mick was a builder by trade who lost half his foot in an accident with a cement mixer. He wore an apron, the same apron he had been wearing all weak. It hung over his large stomach. He had not shaved today and was suffering from a 'hang over' after a heavy drinking session the night before, celebrating Crystal Palace Football Club's victory over Manchester United. He had a cigarette in the corner of his mouth with half an inch of ash hanging from it. Most ash simply spilled down his apron or worse still, into the food he was preparing for customers.

You could get a mug of tea, eggs, bacon, sausages, and beans all served with thick white sliced bread and butter. It was cheap, greasy, and hot. Each Formica covered table not only supported half full bottles of tomato sauce, salt, and pepper, but also a century's worth of grease. His food was crude but popular with the locals when served with a steaming hot mug of strong tea.

Ricky ordered two breakfasts and sat opposite Jason. He looked serious for once.

"I'm gonna introduce you to Kelvin Kissinger later. He's a good guy. Look after you he will. Just don't ever cross him," Ricky warned while tipping some salt into his hand and throwing it over his shoulder for luck.

"I won't cross him, if he can get me a job. What sort of job would it be?" Jason asked.

Ricky paused and looked around the room before leaning forward and whispering.

"Em, well that's up to Ricky." He paused again and squeezed a spot on his cheek. "Some things you may not like. I've done it, but now that I'm older I do other jobs. Just do as you're told and think of the money you'll make. He's gonna like you." Ricky smiled, wiping the pus from his spot onto his jeans.

*

Ricky thumped on a black door. It was the back of an adult strip club. The door opened, and a woman who looked nearly sixty with a cigarette hanging from the corner of her mouth looked out.

"Oh, it's you." She sneered, and opened the door fully to allow the boys in.

"Hello, darling. How are yer? Have you missed me?" Ricky grinned.

"Missed you and your cocky face like a hole in me bloody head. Don't walk on that side I just mopped the floor."

"I love it when you talk dirty to me, Sharon. Me and you should get it on and run away together to a tropical island." Ricky joked.

"What have you been bloody smoking? Tropical island my arse. I got to clean this place and wouldn't you know it, some punter threw up in the gents bathroom last night. No consideration for me that's gotta clean it." Sharon moaned. Sharon had worked at the club for over thirty years. She originally started as a stripper during the war, ten years later, when she got too old and fat to strip, she became barmaid. Now she was demoted to cleaner.

Ricky walked on ahead. Jason followed, trying to take in his surroundings. The club smelt of cigarettes and stale beer. Ricky went into a door behind the bar. On his way, he picked up a bag of crisps. After a steep flight of stairs, he walked down a hallway.

"Mr. Kissinger, I got another recruit for you. He cost me breakfast," Ricky said with his hand raised out.

"Well, it looks like you helped yourself to the crisps, so we can call it quits," Kissinger snapped. He looked up and saw Jason following. "That's the third boy this week. What is it with you? I need girls. I got bloody boys coming out my ears. Still, very nice, come here," he said looking at Jason.

Kissinger was a lot younger than Jason had expected. In his late twenties, he had long hair and a thick moustache. He wore faded denim jeans and a black Led Zeppelin T-shirt. On top of that he wore a sleeveless leather waistcoat. Jason walked up to him and held out his hand.

"Very nice, yes very nice, Ricky. Blond and blue eyes. What are you, eleven?" Kissinger asked stroking Jason's hair and walking around and admiring him.

"I'm twelve." Jason smiled at the man.

"I suppose you want somewhere to live, food, and money? You'll be wanting a job, and I suppose you expect Uncle Kelvin to take you in and give you a job," Kissinger asked with a sneer.

"Yes, please, sir." Jason found it hard not to grin. He couldn't believe how lucky he'd been to find this creep, and once he got the chance, he would call SYUL. He was hoping this would put him back in their good books, after the restroom incident.

"Shall I take him to the Chicken Ranch?" Ricky asked.

The what? Jason thought to himself.

"Yes go straight there. I have to make a phone call. I got a special client. We call him *the doctor*." Kissinger took out a small black book from his waistcoat and searched for a phone number.

Ricky held out his hand and waited.

Kissinger noticed it out of the corner of his eye and groaned.

"You kids bleed me dry," he complained as he handed over forty pounds.

Ricky grinned and gave a salute before tugging Jason with him.

"I'm taking you to the Chicken Ranch. You may see me around from time to time, but I don't work there anymore. I'm now a recruiter. You'll be given anything you want. It's like heaven." Ricky smiled as he jumped down the stairs two at a time.

"Am I working on a chicken farm or something?" Jason asked, confused by the terms. Ricky stopped and looked at Jason.

"You daft sod, how can anyone be so bloody green? You'll find out when you get there. They'll give you the best clothing, best food, any games you want," Ricky said, shaking his head.

Jason thought it best not to say anything else. They walked two streets and came to Richmond Mews, a nicer part of Soho in the center of London. The houses were three stories tall with a basement. They stopped at one of the largest homes on Richmond Mews, a three-story double fronted building with a basement. Rather than using the front door, Ricky went down the steps to the lower kitchen door in the basement. In Victorian times, this section was used for staff. He banged on the door and waited.

A woman in her late fifties opened the door. She had blonde hair that was going grey and the largest chest Jason had ever seen. He couldn't help but stare.

"Ricky, come in. So this is the new boy Kelvin just called me about." She smiled and held out her hand to Jason. "Hello, love. Nice to meet ya. I'm Betty, you must be Jason."

"Yeah, Betty as in, *Betty you ain't seen boobs that big*." Ricky laughed. She was fast and smacked him across the side of his head.

"That's enough of your bloody cheek, young man. And you can wipe the smile off your face Jason unless you want a clout," snapped Betty. "Follow me. I'll show you to your room, and you can meet the others.

Betty gave Jason a tour of the basement. The kitchen was huge and full of anything he wanted, cans of Coke, candy and fresh fruit. She took him up the stairs to the living area. In the front room two boys about ten years old were lying on the floor playing Monopoly. A girl no older than eight sat with a doll on her lap, brushing its hair. The TV was on, but no one was watching. Jason thought they all seemed happy. They all said hello. One of the boys asked if Jason would be sharing their room. When Betty said yes, both boys grinned at him.

Chapter Four

Jason made small talk with some of the boys; all of them had run away from home, some had been here for several months. At five in the evening, Betty called them all down for dinner. She served them sausages and mashed potatoes. Jason knew he would soon have to find a way of contacting SYUI, and after listening to the conversations around the dining room table, he had to act fast. Twelve children sat around the long dining table. They laughed and joked. Jason thought they acted somewhat immature for their ages.

He looked across the table at a girl he guessed was around fourteen. She was pretty with large brown eyes and light brown hair tied in ponytails.

"Hi, I'm Jason." He smiled.

She looked at him and seemed annoyed. "Just because you got pretty blue eyes and good looks don't think I'm gonna be your friend *new boy*." She tutted.

Jason grinned at her. "Why? I'm not asking

you out. I just said hi," he croaked. His voice cracked much to his embarrassment. He coughed, trying to clear his throat. His voice seemed to change pitch at will.

She looked down her nose at him and continued. "Huh, as if I would go out if someone under sixteen anyway."

Betty came into the dining room carrying a large bowl of ice cream. "Who wants ice cream?"

"I do," A deep voice replied. It was Kissinger. He strolled into the dining room followed by a man wearing a suit and tie in his forties.

"Uncle Kelvin." A harmonious call came from the children. Jason just looked on.

"Hi kids, hello Jason. I hope you're settling in okay. Denise, good news for you. The doctor has a job for you, so it's goodbye for now. Go with Mr. Spencer up to your room and pack."

The girl Jason had tried to talk to nodded and got up. She smiled at the man and went up stairs. The man who Kissinger called Mr Spencer followed.

Jason stood and turned to Kissinger. "Where are Denise and that man going?" Kissinger glared back at him.

"You ask a lot of questions. You don't need to worry about what others do here. *Nosey.*" He tapped his nose.

Jason paused for a moment. Betty and Kissinger both watched him. He wasn't sure what Denise had to do. Maybe it was harmless, but maybe it wasn't. Either way, he decided now was the time to act. He ran up the stairs after Denise. By the time he made it up the top of the stairs a bedroom door was being closed. He opened it and stormed in.

Denise was putting her clothes in a bag and looked surprised to see him. Spencer looked annoyed. Jason had no time to think. He had to act. He heard Kissinger running up the stairs.

"Jason, what the hell do you think you are doing? This is none of your concern. Get to your room right now," Kissinger shouted.

Jason paused, trying to piece everything together. If he was wrong about his assessment, he would be made to look foolish in the eyes of SYUI. He started to leave the room and stopped while he thought to himself. *But if I'm right, I've got to stop this now.*

He stood on his toes and faced Kissinger. "You sick moron. You sell children to creeps like this doctor character, and we never see them again. This creep's just as bad." He pointed at Mr Spencer.

"Kissinger, what the hell is this? We didn't pay you all that money for this treatment. Deal with it," Mr Spencer protested, his face turning red.

Kissinger made his first mistake; he attempted to grab Jason by his collar. Jason blocked his move and twisted Kissinger's arm behind his back and bent back his fingers. Kissinger screamed out in pain and fell to his knees. Out of the corner of his eye, Jason noticed Spencer coming towards him.

Jason span on his left foot as his right foot catapulted towards the man catching him square on his nose. The blow broke the man's nose and sent him back against the wall. Denise screamed and ran back behind the bed.

Jason ran down the stairs, jumping two at a time. He dodged Betty as she headed up the stairs, then he ran into the room he recognized from earlier as Betty's office. He picked up the phone and called SYUI. While it was ringing Kissinger entered, holding his injured fingers.

"Who are you calling?" he demanded, striding towards Jason.

"*Nosey*," Jason said tapping his nose. He ducked as Kissinger swung a fist at him and came back with a kick to Kissinger's throat. It knocked Kissinger down, temporarily stunning him. Kissinger held his throat and coughed trying to breath. Jason heard a voice coming from the phone.

"I need to speak to George Young or Barbara Inkpen, this is Jason Steed." He panted.

"*The* Jason Steed? We've been looking for you," the operator replied.

"Yes." Jason noticed Kissinger was getting to his feet again and heard footsteps coming down the stairs. "I'm at 243 Mews Gardens. I need assistance

ASAP, and you may want to send an ambulance."

"I got that. It may take longer for SYUI. Do you want the regular police as well?"

"Yes, anyone. Get them here fast," Jason said. He stood back as Betty and Spencer entered the office.

"Okay, help is on its way, Jason. Are you in danger?" the SYUI operator asked.

"No, *they are*," Jason replied before dropping the phone.

Kissinger picked up a chair. Jason stood on the balls of his feet in a fighting stance. His eyes darkened as his pupils dilated. He forced adrenaline into his system. His body started trembling. He blocked out all distractions and focused completely on Kissinger, Betty, and Spencer.

"This isn't my fight; I'm off. And Kissinger, you owe me." As Spencer tried to leave Jason attacked. He leapt forward and elbowed Betty out of the way. Spencer tried to defend himself, but Jason threw two punches into the man's rib cage at terrific speed. For good measure Jason brought his knee up into his victim's groin.

Kissinger swung the chair at Jason. Jason tried to duck back but was caught on the side of the face with the foot of the chair. Jason cursed at Kissinger and attacked. What followed was an onslaught of rapid punches to Kissinger's face. Jason's disadvantage of height and weight was well compensated by his speed and accuracy. Betty attacked Jason with a rolling pin. He blocked it with his foreman, but the weight and momentum sent Jason down on the ground. The blow was painful, and it sent a bolt of pain through Jason's body.

He would never normally hit a woman, but when high adrenaline and in pain, he moved into protection mode. The full roundhouse kick to her stomach sent her across the room and partially through a window. Doctors later told her that it was a miracle that she didn't die of blood lose as the glass almost severed a main artery.

Kissinger staggered to his feet, pulled out a knife, and waved it at Jason. With a move Jason had learnt in Judo class, Kissinger was disarmed. For good measure, Jason broke his arm at the elbow.

Kissinger's chilling scream set panic into the children. Some ran upstairs, some into the street, and some just cowered in a corner. Spencer tried again to get to his feet, but as he did, he looked up and his eyes met Jason's.

"Stay down," Jason growled. The man lay back down on the ground. It was if he could see death in the boy's eyes.

Jason touched the side of his face, it was tender from the foot of the chair, and he was bleeding. Denise and another girl ran screaming into the street as the first police car arrived. She told them that Jason had gone crazy and had hurt her Uncle Kelvin and had thrown Betty through a window.

Two police officers burst into the hallway and came face to face with Jason. One was a tall thin male policeman and the other a policewoman. Jason stood in a stance, ready to protect himself. For a few tense moments nothing happened. Jason panted, his dark eyes staring at the police.

"You need to come outside and tell us what happened son," The policeman suggested. He gently tried to take Jason's arm and escort him outside.

Jason mistook the move as an attack and blocked, taking a step back as he fought to control his temper. *Okay, calm down. These are the good guys,* he told himself.

The stunned policeman rubbed his forearm that had just been hit by Jason's block. "Now, you don't want to do that son if you know what's good for you." He removed his truncheon and waved the ten-inch long heavy weapon at Jason.

Jason took a deep breath and relaxed. For a few years he had been trying to calm himself down after a high adrenaline fight. He knew he had a terrible temper.

"Yes officer. I'm sorry. I thought you were attacking me. I was the one that called you," Jason said softly. He relaxed and leant against a wall. The adrenaline rush had exhausted him. The policeman went to help Betty who was hanging out the window and screaming for help.

Spencer climbed to his feet. "I was just dropping something off. I have to leave." He made his way to the hallway.

"Sir, I'll need a statement first," The policewoman said.

"Eh, my names John Smith," he stuttered. "I have to leave." He tried to make his way to the door.

"Ma'am, I work for SYUI. I called them and they alerted you as first response. No one is leaving until they get here. This guy is called Spencer he works for some guy called the doctor," Jason told her.

She looked at Jason, her mouth opened as if she was going to say something; she was puzzled and made her way to the front door.

"No one is leaving until we find out what happened here," she ordered.

Spencer cursed and made his way back down the hall and sat on the stairs. "I'm not saying anything until I see my lawyer."

The policewoman never spoke to Jason again, she was unsure if he was telling the truth and was not sure what to think of the situation, she decided to wait for back up to arrive and let her seniors take over. More police arrived, Mew Gardens lit up with blue flashing lights and sirens. Police cars, two ambulances, and four black unmarked SYUI cars arrived.

George Young arrived with Barbara Inkpen. The police stepped aside when George and his staff waved their ID cards. George walked past the police and entered the home. He found Jason sat on the floor in the hallway with his head down, resting on his knees.

"Are you okay Jason?" he asked. Jason looked up and forced a smiled. He lifted his hand up, and George pulled him to his feet. Jason took George and Barbara into the kitchen and explained everything to them. George was pleased with the results; Kissinger was arrested although like Betty, was taken to hospital first.

The children were collected by social services. They would all later be given counselling. Many would return home, some would be sent into foster care. Jason gave his statements, the cut on his face was treated, and George personally drove him home.

"Well Jason, here we are again. Another case solved by Jason Steed." George grinned.

"Not exactly, George. We never found Abigail." Jason sighed.

"Oh, she was picked up the same night you disappeared. The Salvation Army reunited her with her parents. She was cold and hungry and very lucky not to have been picked up by Kissinger and his gang.

"So I did this for absolutely nothing?"

"On the contrary. Kissinger was selling some children to a horrid man they called the doctor.

Kissinger will tell us everything, that's the type of weasel he is. He'll try and get a smaller prison sentence for information. This Doctor guy has been selling young body organs to the highest bidder That Spencer is a low life scumbag who works for him. A real nasty piece of work."

"I don't want to think about it. It's sick. They was going to take a pretty girl called Denise. By tomorrow she could have been cut up and killed," Jason said ,screwing up his face like he was about to vomit.

"I know. At least now he won't be able to hurt anyone again, and those kids will all be better off, thanks to you. This is why we preach to children *do not talk to strangers*. You never know what people are like or what they intend."

Chapter Five

Two days later, Jason walked across the schoolyard, surrounded by hundreds of boys close to his own age. They were all heading in the same direction, all wearing the same black jackets, white shirts, and mauve tie, all of them thinking probably the same thoughts.

Jason's tie was purposefully crooked. His long, blond bangs fell over his face. So why did he feel so out of it, as if he were watching from someone else's eyes? He had missed school for a week and was working hard to catch up. His teachers had not been sympathetic. None said much, even when he handed them a note from a doctor. (SYUI had invented the story that he'd been sick with stomach cramps and diarrhoea.) They smiled and nodded and secretly thought of him as a little spoilt and pampered.

And he couldn't tell the truth. He was never allowed to tell anyone what had really happened, apart from Scott of course.

It had been nearly two years since he had started St Joseph's. He had used his Martial Arts skills just once in his first year when some older boys were trying to put a fellow first-year boy's head down a toilet. Jason intervened and saved Scott Turner. Since that day, Scott had been his best friend they were almost like brothers.

As time passed however, memories had faded. More and more boys had purposely bumped into Jason in a corridor. One boy made a remark about Scott and Jason being a little too close for just friends. Each time, Jason had turned the other cheek, but his frustration with school life was causing his patience to run thin.

This morning was a Wednesday, which meant gym class. The boys all had to go and play soccer. All the boys that was, except for Jason. He took an extra language class. The school agreed that he could count his karate and Judo lessons he did outside of school as his physical education. As lunchtime rolled around, Jason met up with Scott in the canteen.

"You look frozen," Jason said.

"It was bloody cold out on the pitch today. I hate football. It's not fair you get to miss it." Scott shivered.

"I do enough sports. You have to do something, Scott; you can't just exercise your brain. Your body needs to work out as well."

"Work out? I was so blue with cold when I came in and went to take a shower, when I looked in the mirror I saw a Smurf looking back at me!"

Jason roared with laughter. He had trouble keeping the food in his mouth. A bread roll hit him on the back of the head he turned and looked. Malcolm Vango was grinning at him, his group of friends laughed as well.

Vango had been tormenting Scott for some time and had been getting more brazen regarding pushing Jason. Most people avoided Vango. His father was a wealthy man. Rumours circulated that his father was a crook. He never worked but had a large home, always had new cars, and when he paid for Malcolm's school fees, he brought cash in a briefcase.

Vango was well built, with a turned-up nose and black, slightly greasy hair that hung down to his collar. He made a point of ensuring his tie was never straight and slouched around with his hands in his pockets and an attitude that warned everyone, even staff, to keep his distance. There was arrogance to him that Jason and Scott could feel a hundred feet away. The fact that Jason wasn't scared of him only angered him all the more.

"What are you staring at, Steed? Fancy me, do ya? Getting tired of your boyfriend?" Vango joked.

Jason turned away and faced his food again.

"See I told you he's yella. I bet he don't really know karate and Judo. He's a wimp just like his nerd boyfriend. Just look at Steed's hair, what boy has their hair that long in the front you can't see his eyes half the time? I bet he wears a dress at home."

Vango laughed.

"Come on Jason, let's go. I'm not hungry. He's not worth it," Scott said. He could tell that Vango was getting to his friend. Jason had gone quiet. He was worried what Jason would do to the kid.

Jason looked up though his long blond bangs at Scott. "Yeah, your right," Jason said quietly. Both he and Scott got up and started to leave.

"Brawk, buk, buk, buk, buk," Vango crowed like a chicken. Scott was about to put his tray back, but instead he turned and walked over to Vango. To everyone's surprise, he smashed Vango across the face with it.

Jason watched open mouthed. He had never seen Scott so much as hurt a fly before, and now he had just smashed a tray over the schools biggest loud mouth and bully in front of the entire school.

The blow knocked Vango of his chair, his lunch spilling over him. A few laughed at the incident, more just gasped. Vango leapt to his feet, cursing at the top of his voice. Scott ran to Jason for protection. The usual chatter and hum of so many voices that normally echoed all around went silent.

"That was awesome." Jason laughed. "Way to go, Scott. You do have some guts in you. Now what's your plan? Vango and three of his goons are coming."

Scott was turning white and visibly shaking.

"Um. Jase mate, help me out here," Scott stuttered, trying to hide behind his friend.

Jason stepped forward, still laughing. That made matters worse. Vango stood a foot away from Jason and pointed at Scott.

"That little nerd is going down, and if you don't move I'll go through you," Vango growled at Jason.

Jason slightly raised himself on the soles of his feet. He twisted his body at an angle to reduce his size as a target.

Don't hurt them. They're just schoolboys, Jason told himself.

"And what do we have here? Fighting is it?" Mr. Griffiths, the headmaster, bellowed from down the corridor. "Vango, Steed my office *now*."

Jason sulked on his way home. The sun was already dipping behind his home, but daylight still lingered in the air as if accidently left behind. As he slammed the large black iron gates hard enough that they bounced open again. Jason hesitated, debating whether to go back and close them, then gave up on the idea. As he walked up the long gravel drive towards his stately white house surround by acres of grass and mature Oaks he grew angry. He knew he would be in trouble with his father.

Jason was always in a bad mood unless Scott was with him, but today was much worse. His father normally put it down to his age and expected it may get a little worse when he became a teenager. Today, he was so angry he was physically shaking. It would be the first time his father had heard his son curse.

The front door slammed shut behind him. The usual pattern of throwing his school bag across the floor and kicking his shoes off in all directions was followed up with a loud sigh.

"Hi Jason, how was school?" his father asked.

Jason marched up to his father and pulled out a letter from his pocket and threw it at is father. "I have been suspended from that dump for a week." He cursed.

Ray was surprised by Jason's language. He knew Jason disliked school, but wasn't going to let him get away with cursing.

"What did you say?"

"Read the note." He cursed again.

"Get to your room," Ray shouted.

Jason turned and walked up to his room. He watched his father out of the corner of his eye. He knew the routine. His father would follow him up, removing his belt, and he would get spanked. Jason paused at the top of the stairs. When he looked down at his father, Ray stood at the bottom of the stairs just watching his son.

Jason gave the same look he gets from his father when he is asked a question; he raised his eyebrows and stared. It was what Scott called the

'Steed asking a question look.'

"You know Jason, maybe you're too old to be spanked now. We seem to do much better just talking about your problems. Let's start with the first problem. Why are you suspended from school?"

Jason sighed and sat on the top step, looking down at his father. "Okay, don't get mad. I never so much as touched anyone, but I was suspended for fighting."

"Who?" His father asked. He walked up the stairs and sat next to his son on the top stair.

"That idiot with the motor mouth, Malcolm Vango."

"Vango as in Mick Vango's boy, the mobster?" Ray asked.

"Yeah."

"How bad did you hurt him?" Ray sighed, dreading the worst.

"I never laid a finger on him. I know better than to fight in school. It was Scott. He smashed a tray into his face. You should have seen it, it was awesome. Then he ran behind me for protection." Jason laughed. "Just as Vango was coming to kill Scott, Taffy Griffiths came around the corner, saw us standing toe to toe, Vango's got blood, snot, and food all over his face, and Taffy thinks we were fighting. Vango is suspended too."

"Well why didn't you explain that to Mr.

Griffiths?"

"Derrr. Scott's my best friend. I can't grass him up," Jason rudely replied. Ray attempted to smack Jason across the back of the head, but Jason instinctively and rapidly reacted and blocked it.

"Gosh, you're fast son," Ray said. "But less of your cheek. I'm your father, not a kid from school. Don't *derrr* me again. So because you don't want to grass on Scott, you get suspended and a bad school record?"

"Well actually, Scott was saving me too. Vango was taunting me, throwing bread at me, calling me yellow, and saying crude stuff about mine and Scott's friendship. Scott knew it was only a matter of time before I cracked and busted Vango's head open, so he did it with a tray. Let's face it, if I had touched him I would get an assault charge." Jason grinned. "I'm quite proud of Scott. He's grown some balls at last. Before today I always thought Scott in a fight would be about as useful as a woodpecker with a rubber beak."

Ray said nothing as he watched his son smile. He still had the same adorable cheeky grin. His white teeth glistened, and his sapphire blue eyes sparkled.

"You're not happy at school, are you son?"

"I hate it Dad. I enjoy learning the languages, chatting to Scott, but after going on missions, car chases, shooting guns and having some great fights, school just sucks. Even the last mission, I got to kick the stuffing out of some sickos. In school, I have to read huge thick books written by some guy who has been dead for a hundred years or add up x=y+2. Who cares about that stuff, well apart from Scott?"

Ray placed his arm around his son's shoulders and kissed him on the forehead. "Do you also think you can curse at me?"

"Em. No. I'm sorry about that, Dad. I was in a bad mood," Jason said. He flashed his eyes at his father and grinned. "Am I forgiven?"

"No." Ray caught Jason in a headlock and tickled him until he screamed for mercy.

*

Jason watched the buildings flash by. It was a three-hour drive to the Royal Navy command headquarters in Portsmouth. Jason's father drove a fraction over the speed limit as he always did. He wore his naval uniform and had made Jason wear his Sea Cadet uniform. When Jason had asked why they were going, he simply told Jason he would find out, and it was probably something he would like.

Jason assumed his father, who was a second Lieutenant, was being promoted to Captain, like his friend Bill Giles. Jason thought that he deserved a ship of his own to command now and was proud of him. He had noticed his father had closed his office door a few times while he had been on the phone, something he had never done before.

The drive was uneventful. Jason had broken

the knob on the radio. Ray Steed had switched it to Radio Two for older songs, and Jason kept switching to Radio One for pop songs and made yawning noises when Radio Two was on. In a small struggle to control the station, the knob broke off. Now the radio was stuck on a farming channel. Worse still, they couldn't turn it off. They had to listen to two hours of how to prevent pigs from getting mange mites and how to cure a fungi problem on Elm trees.

When they stopped at the Royal Naval headquarters, an armed guard dressed in Sailors uniform approached the car.

Ray wound down his window. "Commander Raymond Steed here to see Admiral Neville Hollyingberry."

The guard saluted and looked at Ray's ID. He looked across at Jason and passed the ID back. "Go straight in, sir."

Ray drove through the opened gate and noticed Jason was grinning. "What's so funny?"

"Dad, you put on your posh voice when you said that, one is here to see Admiral Neville Hollyingberry," Jason said putting on an upper crust accent.

Ray looked annoyed, and then smiled. "Best behaviour, Jason," Ray ordered.

"I'm gonna laugh if you talk like that again. I can't help it." Jason smirked. "How long are you going to be seeing him for? Can I have a look around the base?"

"No, you're coming with me."

Jason's smirk disappeared. He had only met a Captain before, and that was Bill and he was a family friend. Jason knew Admiral Hollyingberry was Admiral of the fleet, the head of the Royal Navy.

Chapter Six

After a brief, wait Ray and Jason were shown into a conference room. Jason took in his surroundings—large pictures of Naval ships dressed the walls, and portraits of previous Admirals, going back to Admiral Nelson, hung from one wall. Three men sat at the table, one in uniform who Jason guessed was Admiral Hollyingberry, a slim grey haired man in a suit with a smile that looked fake to Jason, and a larger man in a black suit with his back to them.

Ray and Jason stopped and saluted.

The Admiral saluted back and stood from his seat. "And you must be Sea Cadet Jason Steed. I'm pleased to finally meet you young man. I have heard so much about you, although I expected you to be bigger." Hollyingberry smiled and shook Jason's hand. He looked at Ray and shook his hand. "This is Wallace Peters from the Ministry and you know George Young of course."

Jason looked wide-eyed. "George. Em, hi, I never, em, what are you doing here?" Jason asked looking over his shoulder to see his father's reaction.

"All in good time Jason, take a seat. Would you like some tea?" Hollyingberry asked.

Jason watched as a naval steward poured four cups of tea into fine china cups. He looked at George still wide-eyed and back at his father. He was trying to work out what was going to happen next; this wasn't what he had expected.

She looked at Jason. "What will you drink?" she asked.

"I'll have a Coke please."

"A repulsive drink. I've always thought. I've never understood the taste unless mixed with a little rum. But of course you shall have what you want," Hollyingberry said.

The stewardess quickly paced to the fridge and brought a Coke for Jason. He was surprised he was being treated so well, something seemed out of place he thought. Wasn't his father the guest of honour?

"I'll explain, shall I?" Wallace asked, gently placing his cup back in the saucer and wiping his lips with a tissue. "Jason, we at the ministry have been concerned about you. I've been talking to the Admiral, your father, your school, and George Young. You've proven yourself over and over again." He paused. "Although you seem to be having some problems at school and let's face it, St Josephs is one of Britain's finest schools."

"Yes, if you're a nerd," Jason said much to the

amusement of George who had to cough to conceal his laugh.

"We are aware that being on an undercover mission and having assassins attacking you one moment then going back to school and being told not to run down the corridor the next must be very difficult for you. That's why we have come up with the idea of sending you to QRMA," Wallace said.

"QR... What, where?" Jason asked. He looked at his father. Ray reassuringly placed his hand on Jason's knee.

Wallace continued. "Quentin Roosevelt Military Academy. It's in South Dakota in the United States. It's for students aged twelve to eighteen. The US has over seventy Military Academies; they take students from age eleven. The best of each of those schools are tested after the first year. Twenty-five, that's less than one student from every two academies, make it to QRMA, so only the very best. Let's face it, Jason, you're the perfect candidate for a military school. Unfortunately, we don't have any in the UK. If we did, we're sure you would be top in your class. We've arranged with the US to send you to the Quentin Roosevelt Military Academy. In exchange, they wish to send two US Marines to train with the Royal Marines."

Jason sat quietly, trying to take it all in while gently sipping his Coke.

"Have you heard of Quentin Roosevelt? Do you know who he was?" Hollyingberry asked.

"Yes sir, he was an American President," Jason said.

"No, Jason. He was the son of President Theodore Roosevelt. He was an ace fighter pilot in World War One; he died aged twenty-one when his plane was shot down in a dogfight. The academy is named after him. It has a reputation of being the toughest military school in the world. Two US presidents and a total of ten, four star Generals all went to QRMA," Hollyingberry explained.

"How long do I have to go for?" Jason asked.

The question wasn't answered. The room fell silent until Ray eventually spoke.

"It will be your new school son. You'll be enrolled until you are eighteen, just like you are at St. Josephs. You'll board at the school and come home on term breaks and recess," Ray said.

Jason bit his bottom lip. He wanted to ask more. How could he continue with Karate and Judo or see Catherine and Scott? For now, he kept the thoughts to himself.

"There are a few points I have to make Jason," Wallace explained. "First of all, you must control that temper of yours. George filled us in on the Paddington station incident. I also understand you have been suspended from school for fighting. You'll be representing Great Britain; we will not tolerate any of that nonsense. The second point is more important. You'll be given access to the top US military academy, you will be roommates and classmates with future American leaders. You will also have access to many places that no other country can get within five miles." Wallace paused and sipped his tea.

"Although the US are our allies we may from time to time ask you to keep an eye open and an ear to the ground. Do I make myself clear?" Wallace stiffened.

"I never agreed to that. Jason is a perfect fit for a military school, and that's what he's doing. He is not on another mission," Ray said.

"It's not a mission, Ray. We just want a report, that's all," George said. "We have people in the US who will make contact with Jason."

Jason sat quietly, feeling miserable. He looked at his father. "I thought we were coming here today because you was getting promoted, getting your own ship." The room fell into an awkward silence. Jason eventually broke it and faced Hollyingberry. "Yes, sir. I will do Great Britain proud."

George faked a cough and spoke. "On another bright note Jason, we caught the person they called 'The Doctor' and rescued three more children. He is actually a surgeon from Great Ormands Street in London and was selling human organs to rich people who needed body parts. He also carried out heart transplants. You saved many lives with your actions. Well done."

"George, are you forgetting your department

is being investigated for excessive force? I think a total of four people were hospitalized after that mission," Wallace barked.

"Jason got the job done and put the bad guys away. No more children will get hurt thanks to him. I can deal with the paperwork and all the hassle that follows," George said.

Jason said three words on the entire journey home. One was "no" when asked if he wanted a drink and "not hungry" when asked if he wanted to stop to eat. Once they arrived home Ray let him spend a few hours alone before trying to talk to him again. He knew his son would have more questions and concerns.

"You don't have to go. You can stay here and continue at St. Josephs or you can go to the world's top military academy. You choose Jason," Ray said.

"Of course I want to go to the American military academy, but I'll miss Catherine, Scott and—" Jason paused, his eyes filled with tears. "I'll miss you." Ray hugged his son. Jason's exterior toughness always collapsed when it came to the love for his father.

Chapter Seven

Explaining to Princess Catherine he was going to school in America, which meant they would hardly see each other, went easier than he had expected. They had a strange friendship. She considered him her boyfriend and he called her his girlfriend. But they had not been able to spend much time together, and the time they had been together it was usually for a family birthday celebration. They never had time alone to talk and had become little more than friends.

Scott, on the other hand, had been difficult. Scott's large brown eyes welled up. The two boys had become very close and shared a brotherly love. Scott was concerned how Jason would cope with his homework without him. Jason was concerned that the likes of Malcolm Vango would bully Scott once he wasn't there to protect him. Though Jason did thump Scott for saying he would take Catherine out on a date while Jason was away.

He was given instructions to travel in his Sea Cadet uniform. He had already sent ahead his measurements, so his new uniforms would be provided once he arrived, but it was a rule he came in his existing uniform.

*

May 1st 1975.

Ray took Jason to London's Heathrow airport and found it difficult saying goodbye to his son. It would be two months before Jason returned and very likely that he would be away at sea when Jason came home. He was leaving himself in a few days to join the Royal Navy's aircraft carrier, HMS Hermes. The housekeeper, Mrs. Beeton, would look after Jason or he would spend time with his grandparents in Scotland. They kissed goodbye and hugged. Jason walked through to the departure lounge and found himself with mixed feelings, both nervous and excited.

The nine-hour flight on a United States Boeing 747 was over much quicker than Jason expected. His stomach tightened as the plane touched down at Des Moines International Airport. He collected his bags, went through a military passport control, and noticed a solider holding a small board with the name Jason Steed written across it.

Jason approached him and saluted. "Jason Steed, sir." Jason thought the solider was around twenty. He still had acne on his face. Peterson was written on his shirt breast pocket. Jason assumed that was his surname.

"Follow me and keep up." Peterson grunted, turned, and marched towards an exit. Jason jogged behind, struggling to keep up while carrying his suitcase and shoulder bag. Peterson climbed into a military Jeep and started the engine. Jason threw his bags in the back. As soon as he lifted himself in, the Jeep sped off before Jason was sat down.

"Hi, I'm Jason." Jason smiled.

"No, here you will be called Steed. I'm Peterson and pissed off. I never joined the army to chauffer snotty little rich kids around."

So much for the friendly welcome, Jason thought to himself. "Then why *did* you join the US army?"

"To defend my country. Fight for our freedom."

"You are. I thought some of the best US generals went to Quentin Roosevelt Military Academy. Do you help run the place?"

"Yeah, they turned out some good generals and a few president's, but many of the students are spoilt little rich kids like you. No offence, but really what's the point of sending a pretty boy like you here? I bet your family is loaded too."

Jason frowned at Peterson. He wanted to argue, tell him that no wonder he was just a driver if he had that attitude. He chose to say nothing and enjoy the American scenery. The two hundred mile drive from Iowa to Quentin Roosevelt Military Academy in South Dakota took them almost four hours. Jason marvelled at the large cars and trucks, the long straight roads with motels and diners scattered along the route, scenes that he had only seen in movies.

The Jeep stopped at a guardhouse, an eight-foot high fence surrounded a large complex. It was dark, so Jason couldn't quite make out the buildings. He was dropped off and told to go to the main building and report to Corporal Jones.

He struggled with his bags across the parade ground and headed to the largest building where the doorway was lit up. Jason inhaled deeply as he entered. It reminded him of HMS Raleigh, a British Naval base. The scent made him feel more at home. He knocked on the door marked Corporal Jones.

"Enter," a voice from within said. Jason entered. The office was clean and orderly. A man in his early forties in a green US army blazer sat at a desk full of exercise books. Jason dropped his bags and saluted.

"Jason Steed, sir. I was told to report to Corporal Jones."

Corporal Jones looked Jason up and down. "So you're the Brit. Not what I expected. You seem a little small for the top seventh grade military candidate in Britain. You're twelve?"

"Yes, sir. I turned twelve in March."

"Your classmates are from all over the country. The best from each state's military schools. I see by your uniform you were a Sea Cadet?"

"No, sir. I mean, yes sir. But I'm still a Sea Cadet," Jason stuttered.

"Not anymore, Steed. Your new uniform will be in your room. Now you're a US Army Cadet. If you graduate, when you're eighteen you can choose from he Army, Navy, Royal Marines, Coast Guard, or Air force." He looked at Jason and pointed. "What are those ribbons on your chest, merit badges?"

"No, sir. One is the Victoria Cross and the other is the Queen's Award for Bravery." Jason smiled and proudly stuck out his chest.

The corporal frowned at Jason. "In the United States. you can only wear a medal that you are awarded. Don't tell me you were awarded them."

"Yes sir, I was. I was a survivor in the Jakarta Massacre. The Queen awarded them to me in a private ceremony."

"Really?" Corporal Jones smiled and saluted Jason. "We heard all about the massacre of the Sea Cadets. We heard a few survived. One even escaped with a cassette we had that armed a nuclear warhead. The survivors where very lucky. I can see why they sent you here now. It's an honour to meet you, Private Steed." He came around his desk and shook Jason's hand.

Something he said puzzled Jason but he couldn't quite put his finger on it, so he ignored it.

Chapter Eight

Corporal Jones marched up the stairs with Jason following behind. Jones was over six foot with large legs so he took the stairs two at a time. Jason battled with his bags to keep up with him. He followed the man along a corridor, with rows of doors either side.

Jones explained, “This floor is reserved for year one as far as Quentin Roosevelt Military Academy is concerned or 8th grade as you're probably used to. All students on this floor are aged twelve to thirteen. Next year if you're still here, you'll go up a level.” He stopped and waited for Jason to catch up. “Here we are room twenty-five.” He knocked on the door.

A boy with red hair opened the door. Jason thought he was about twelve, maybe thirteen; he wore just his Pajama bottoms, his mouth full of frothy white paste and a toothbrush. He saluted when he noticed Corporal Jones; he stood back and allowed them both in.

“This is Private Luttrell. He's been here, like most of the other students on this floor, for eight months. You're behind all of them so you'll need to play catch up." He looked at Luttrell. "You have a new responsibility. Show Private Steed around and let him know how things work. If he gets lost or screws up I'll blame you." He saluted, stamped his heels, and marched out of the room.

Jason held out his hand, but Luttrell ignored it and dashed to a sink and spat out his mouthful of toothpaste. Jason took in his surroundings of the dorm room. It had bunk beds; the lower bunk had bedding folded neatly and had some uniforms laid out. The top bunk looked like it had been slept in. There were posters on the walls of air force fighter planes, bombers, and an aircraft carrier.

On one wall a huge flag was hung. Jason looked at it; it was three colors—red, white, and blue with a white star in the center of a blue vertical stripe. The room had a sink that Luttrell was rinsing his mouth in plus two wardrobes and two desks side by side.

After Luttrell wiped his mouth dry with the back of his hand, he came forward and shook Jason's hand. "I heard I was getting a roommate today, but once it got past nine I doubted you were coming. I'm Seth, Seth Luttrell." He smiled and noticed Jason was looking at his flag. "Beautiful isn't it?"

Jason looked up at the flag. "I'm Jason Steed. What country is it?"

The boy looked annoyed by the question. "What country do you think it is?"

Jason paused. This kid was obviously proud of his country; he didn't want to upset his new roommate. "Em, you know Seth, I'm not really good at geography, as a guess I would say *Cuba*?"

Luttrell laughed and then cursed. "The Cubans are communists their flag is." He paused and ran to his briefcase and pulled out a book. He fingered through the pages. "Ah here, Cuba. Okay, I'll let you off it's similar. But if you don't want to get hurt you better not make that mistake again. It's the mighty flag of Texas, and there are lots of us Texans here so do yourself a favor and don't make that mistake again. Besides, where are you from? You sound Australian?"

"I'm British. Well I was born in Hong Kong, but my mother was Scottish and my father is English. He's a commander in the Royal Navy on an aircraft carrier."

"British, cool. Which one?" Luttrell asked. He went to a desk and pulled out another book, this one with ships on the cover.

"Oh, HMS Hermes." He joined Luttrell looking for a picture of it. "So, do I call you Seth or Luttrell?" Jason asked.

"Tex or Luttrell works for me. Most of our class call me Tex. The teachers call me Luttrell. Here it is, HMS Hermes. Oh it's a baby just seven hundred and seventy feet. The USS Nimitz that comes into service next month is over one thousand feet long."

"Well, you know what they say about a man

who drives a big car. He's compensating for a small..." Jason joked. Tex squinted at Jason; he never got the joke. Jason remembered Scott informing him that the Americans had a different sense of humour. Maybe this was what he meant.

They spent a few hours talking, but eventually Jason had to climb into his bunk. He was jet lagged. He hadn't eaten but was confident breakfast would be good. It was past midnight and Tex had his alarm set for six in the morning.

It seemed that no sooner had his head hit the pillow the alarm was going off.

Jason met most of his class in the bathroom just after six. The large room was full of chatter. He received several looks when he stepped into the shower. He assumed it was because he was the new boy.

Tex stayed close to him, making sure he never got lost and found his way back to their dorm room.

"They let you wear your hair that long in the front in the British Sea Cadets?" Tex asked as he watched Jason gel his long blond fringe back over his head.

"No, not really, I gel it back. I keep the back and sides short. It's called a Hitler Youth cut since it's how they wore their hair. I like my fringe long," Jason said.

"Your fringe?" Seth asked.

"Yeah, this." Jason pointed to the blond hair hanging over his eyebrows.

"That's your bangs." Tex grinned.

Jason pulled on his new uniform. He found it strange to be wearing a jacket with the American flag on his shoulder. He looked around the room, holding the plastic it came wrapped in.

"Where's the bin?" Jason asked.

"The, what did you say, *bin*?"

"Yeah the bin to put the rubbish in. You know, a rubbish bin."

Tex roared with laughter. "Jason, you'll have to learn to speak English. You mean a trashcan. We don't have them in the rooms because guys were putting food scraps in them. The place was infested with cockroaches. All trash goes in the trash cans in the bathrooms, and they're emptied twice a day."

They walked down to the canteen together. Jason was impressed with the canteen, although he was told it was called a mess hall not a canteen. They offered everything to eat except hot tea. As he tucked into eggs and bacon, he looked at Tex.

"What do you want to join when you're eighteen, Navy?"

"Hell no. The US Marines. What about you?" Tex asked.

"S.A.S.," Jason said.

"S.A.S? What's that?"

"Em, Special Air Service. Like your Navy Seals, but tougher and smarter," he automatically and proudly said without thinking.

Tex's face changed. "Bull, no one is tougher than the US Naval Seals. You Brits wouldn't stand a chance against them. We sent you home running in 1776 and took the country for ourselves in the revolution."

"Ha, that was a civil war and we let you have it. We still had India, Australia, Hong Kong, and Canada. Even today Hawaii has the British Union Jack as part of its flag. We let you share it with the Native Indians." Jason grinned.

"Oh boy, you're gonna be a hoot in history, and we got that first lesson with Corporal Armstrong. He's the strictest, meanest teacher we have. He's gonna roast you if you mention that." Tex laughed.

Chapter Nine

At seven-thirty they had roll call on the parade ground. It was followed by drill and inspection. Jason had experienced drill in the Sea Cadets, and he found it no more difficult here.

He followed Tex into the first class. He was still getting looks from some of the other students. Many had said hello to him and asked him if he was Australian. He sat next to Seth two rows from the front.

The door flew open and was slammed shut by an overweight man bulging out of his uniform. He turned and faced his students as if he was inspecting them and stood behind his desk at the front of the class. Jason noticed his nametag said *Armstrong* and assumed it was the corporal Seth had warned him about.

"Stand for the Pledge," He ordered.

Jason stood with everyone else; he copied them when they all put their right hands across their hearts and faced the flag in the corner of the room. As they started to say the pledge he stood quiet, looking around and taking in the new experience.

When they had finished they sat down, all that was, except for Corporal Armstrong. He threw a stick of chalk at Jason, who noticed it and caught it in his hand, much to the annoyance of Armstrong. A few gasps went around the room. No one had ever caught the chalk before, or tried. It usually just hit you in the face or head.

"Stand and tell me your name, Private," Barked Armstrong.

"Steed sir. Jason Steed..." He paused. "Em, Private Steed, Sir."

"Well Private Steed. You will now say the Pledge of Allegiance again for us all to hear."

Jason colored up a little, He hated being center of attention and could feel everyone's eyes watching him. He placed his hand on his heart and looked at the flag. Nothing came from his mouth.

"He's new, Sir," Tex said.

Armstrong threw a stick of chalk at him, although he was not fast enough to catch it, and it bounced off his forehead, leaving a white mark. "Did I ask your opinion Luttrell?" Armstrong sneered.

"No, Sir."

"Then get out here and give me fifty."

Tex climbed up from his seat, walked to the front of the class, and performed fifty push-ups. Jason watched, not sure what was going to happen next. He was confident he could do push-ups if he had to. Armstrong turned his attention back to Jason.

"So new boy, did they not do the Pledge at your last school?"

"No, Sir," Jason said.

Armstrong marched towards Jason and faced him. He looked down at Jason, his face just inches away. "Do you take me for a fool boy? What kind of school doesn't do the Pledge of Allegiance every morning?"

"A British school, Sir," Jason said. Some giggles went around the room.

Armstrong pulled away from Jason, his eyes darting around the room trying to see who dared laugh. "Well then Limey. You will be saying the Pledge of Allegiance in class every morning until I say different, and if you get one word wrong, the whole class gets to do fifty." Armstrong smiled. He turned and walked back to his desk feeling sorry for himself. He stopped short and faced Jason again who had sat back down.

"Did I say sit?"

"Um, no sir, sorry sir, I thought..." Jason stuttered and stood again.

"So Limey, name me ten Presidents. They don't have to be in order," Armstrong asked. Most of the class rolled their eyes. They could all answer over twenty but had no confidence in the new boy.

"Well we have President Ford, President Nixon, Washington, Roosevelt." He paused thinking hard, the entire class trying to mouth the names to him. "Oh, President Lincoln, Eisenhower, Em." A long pause followed. "I don't know anymore, Sir."

"Six. You can just name six out of a possible thirty-seven don't they teach history in Britain Private Steed, or are they *all* backward?" Armstrong asked.

The remark angered Jason who was very proud of his country. "Yes sir, they do teach history and much more of it ,as we have so much. Such as all the kings and queens and all the little countries we've owned from time to time, like America. Plus all the wives of King Henry VIII. I doubt anyone here could name them all including you," Jason said.

"Good, Private Steed, very good. So you're proud of your country?" Armstrong asked. "Would put your country before America?"

"Yes, sir. I am proud of my country. I like America. You're our allies, but I would put my country first," Jason said. He watched Armstrong slowly approach him.

Armstrong saluted him. "That is the correct answer, Private Steed. You should be proud of your country. You may sit down, but you still need to learn the Pledge of Allegiance." Armstrong smiled. He took an instant liking to Jason. He admired someone with fire in his belly.

Tex and many of the others looked on open

mouthed. They had never seen Armstrong smile before or known anyone stick up for himself in front of him.

At lunch, Jason and Tex joined three others from class. They all smiled when Jason sat down. "Hi Limey, I'm Austin, but I'm from New York so everyone called me Yankee." Jason shook his hand. The boy was African American and very tall for his age.

"How old are you?" Jason asked.

"Twelve. We're all twelve, except for Cowboy. He's thirteen," Yankee said.

"Howdy, Limey. I'm cowboy, the oldest and toughest in class." He reached over and shook Jason's hand. He was a skinny kid with a face full of acne. His hair was cut so short he almost looked bald.

"Hi. Do you all have nick names?" Jason asked, trying to make a mental note of the names. "Why Cowboy?"

"Cause he's bow legged, looks like he's been riding a horse." Yankee laughed.

"Riding a cow more like, " Tex joked.

"I'm bow legged cause of what I got packed between them," Cowboy joked, making a rude gesture with his hands.

"No, I seen ya in the shower." Yankee laughed, wriggling his little finger at him.

Jason was enjoying his new school. He still had math and was a complete mess in American history, but was more advanced in French and German. He enjoyed the military activates like target practice, map reading, Morse code, and survival training.

By the next morning, he had mastered the Pledge of Allegiance and said it at the front of the class. English was a little difficult. Corporal Jones taught the class. He asked Jason to come to the front of the class and threw him a stick of chalk, so he could see for himself exactly what Armstrong had described in the staff room. Jason caught it easily.

"Private Steed, as you're English I expect you should be good in the lesson, but you'll actually struggle a little with spelling," Jones said.

"I don't think so, Sir. I'm average at punctuation and spelling. I think I can spell no better or worse than anyone else here," Jason said. He was unsure of the question or where Jones was going with it.

"I see., Well then Jason, write down the following on the blackboard. Color, Tire, Center, Program, Yogurt, Labor, and favorite, and Pajamas,." Jones instructed.

Jason confidently started writing the words on the board. By the time he got to the third word he heard gasps from his classmates behind him. He paused stepped back and looked at his spelling, and when he was happy he continued. When he had finished he turned around to notice the whole class grinning at him. Yankee was shaking his head from side to side.

"Okay, Steed. Sit down. You got them all wrong. This is how to spell them." Next to Jason's words he spelt it the American way.

Jason's English	**Corporal Jones**
Colour	*Color*
Tyre	*Tire*
Centre	*Center*
Yoghurt	*Yogurt*
Favourite	*Favorite*
Pyjamas	*Pajamas*

Jason looked at how Jones had spelt the words differently and blushed.

"Don't look so worried, Steed. You spelt it correctly for an English person, well done. But in the US, we spell words very different. These are just a few. If you spell the English way I won't give you a bad mark."

Jason wrote to his grandparents and told them he was enjoying the Military Academy. Most people were helpful and friendly, and he enjoyed the lessons. He even admitted to Tex that the American versions of spelling seem to make more sense. He hated the nickname 'Limey' but it seemed to stick with him, and he couldn't shake it off.

He enrolled in a martial arts class; he never really expected much. It was taught by Sergeant Hammonds. The class had twenty students, three from Jason's year, the other's all older. It was Taekwondo, where Jason was not only a black belt, but also a 3rd Dan, meaning he was two grades higher than a regular black belt. He had three yellow lines on one end of his belt. The other students watched him as he wrapped his belt around his waist. It also caught the attention of Sergeant Hammonds.

"So you're the new boy. That's an impressive belt." Hammonds smiled. Jason looked up at Hammonds. His own belt was a plain black belt. "Maybe you should teach the class if that is really 3rd Dan?"

"Yes, Sir. Third Dan in Taekwondo. I do study other forms, but this is my highest grade and my personal favorite. I started when I was four. I'm pleased we do Taekwondo here."

After the class ended, Jason continued to work out. Some of the others watched him perform his. Kata's, His body effortlessly moved across the gymnasium with speed and grace. Each kick and punch was timed to perfection, hitting his imaginary opponent. When Jason was performing forms he was at his happiest, his mind focused on every muscle fiber in his body.

Chapter Ten

Tex looked up from his book when Jason returned to the dorm room. Jason was red faced and his hair wet with sweat.

"Looks like you either got your butt kicked or you've been on a five mile march." Tex grinned.

"Neither. Just a good workout." Jason sniffed his armpit. "I better take a shower before bed."

He returned wet a few minutes later with a towel wrapped around his waist. Tex had the window open and was gazing outside. Cold air had filled the room.

"Shut the bloody window. It's freezing in here now." Jason moaned.

Tex turned and laughed. "I love your swear words, Limey. They're so British. Even when you're pissed you sound posh." He gestured Jason towards the window. "Look, the siren has gone off at the Airbase. They've got guards running around, search lights, dogs barking. It's probably a drill. I doubt the Russians are invading."

Jason peered out the window with Tex. He wrapped his arms around himself, trying to keep warm. Quentin Roosevelt Airbase was nothing more than an airfield, with modern hangers and large buildings along one side. Yankee had told Jason that is was a research center for the Air Force. Tex and Cowboy argued it was just an old air base. Jason went along with Yankees theory. They had far too much security for just an old base. He thought whatever secrets they had there; they wanted to keep them secret. No one from the Academy had ever been allowed in.

"Okay, now shut the window it's freezing in here," Jason said. He quickly pulled on his Pajamas and climbed into his bed, peering out of the top of his covers.

Tex closed the window, turned off the light, and jumped into his bunk and farted for good measure. "On Saturday we go into town. We normally get malt or a root beer and go to the movies. You'll have to come with us, Limey."

"A malt or a beer? You must think I'm green, no way you guys will get served. You got to be twenty-one here. At least in Britain you can drink at eighteen, but none of you look more that fifteen, even in uniform," Jason said.

"What are you going on about, Limey? A malt shake or a root beer. You don't have to be twenty-one to drink them. It's just milk or soda." Tex laughed. "Don't tell me you have never had a malt or a root beer?"

"Nope. I've had a milkshake. Is it like that?" Jason asked.

"The malt is. The root beer is like Coke but different."

There was still an alert on the airbase. Helicopters came and went; searchlights occasionally lit up the dorm room, as there powerful beam passed. Armed Guards with dogs searched the perimeter.

The following morning, news spread like wild fire in the academy. Someone had broken into the base and two guards had been injured. This caused rumours to spread. Some said it was a pilot going crazy. Others said the Russians were invading. Not even the staff at the academy knew the facts. Security was increased on the airbase, and as a safety measure it was also increased on the adjoining academy.

The incident never stopped the daily arrival of the huge C-9B Skytrain II US Navy Aircraft. The planes flew back and forth from Thailand bringing back used military equipment that was used in the Vietnam War. They were trying to salvage as much as possible. Jason learned that just a few months before a flight contained returning troops, some in body bags.

*

The academy competed each year in the annual US Military School Games. This year was no different. The three-day event would be held at the

US Marine Corps camp in Pendleton, California. The competition was a small version of the Olympic games with just students from Military academies across the US. Quentin Roosevelt Military Academy had a tradition of winning the most medals. They were known as the academy to beat.

The games consisted of sports such as target shooting, assault course time trials, track events, swimming, karate, and a boxing tournament. Jason noticed the list on the wall outside the mess hall. A large grin ran across his face when he read the word karate. He pulled out a pen and scribbled down his name. So far he was the only one in his year who volunteered. Most of the names where from older students.

*

Ten thousand miles away, forces from around the world were employed to oversee events in Vietnam by the United Nations. They became part of the United Nations peacekeeping force. The Americans had pulled out of the American embassy in Saigon, South Vietnam just weeks before, after a long bloody battle that lasted over thirteen years. It cost the lives of over forty seven thousand American troops and wounding over one hundred and fifty thousand. The Vietnamese lost an estimated one million troops and civilians. South Vietnam had now fallen to the North. The United Nations had a task force off shore in the South China Sea.

The French Navy sent the helicopter carrier Jeanne d'Arc and the British Navy sent the aircraft carrier HMS Hermes. This was the same ship Raymond Steed was to rejoin. They operated a joint observation schedule checking the coastal waters. United States President Ford was concerned there would be a massacre by the North Vietnamese communists against the southerners. The United Nations agreed that America would have no part in the observations because of the war that just ended between the two countries.

Chapter Eleven

Three weeks passed and Jason had only written one letter to Princess Catherine. He did send two to Scott who replied with news and updates from his old school. He had not suffered under the hands of Malcolm Vango. Since the tray incident, Scott had been given a new status most boys left him alone.

Jason asked the operator for the international dialling code to England and called his father. The phone was picked up after three rings.

"Steed residence," Ray Steed answered

"Hi, sorry I took so long to call. I've been busy and don't always get time." Jason smiled. There was a long pause.

"Who is this?" his father asked.

"Dad, it's me," Jason replied puzzled.

"Hi, son, sorry. You sound so different. Have you got a cold?"

"Oh that, no. My voice broke." Jason grinned.

"Well, I guess it has. You sound so grown up. You'll be telling me you're shaving next."

"No not quite, Dad. But I am growing hairs under my arms and certain places now."

"Well, how is the Military Academy? Have you made new friends? What's it like?"

"Sure is a sweet place, y'all. I like it here. Gonna get me some goddamn root beer later," Jason said doing his best to speak like his roommate Tex.

Father and son spoke for over fifteen minutes. His father informed him he was lucky to catch him home. In a few hours he would be leaving to join his ship. After the phone call, Jason felt isolated and slightly homesick for a short while but soon had something to occupy him.

The second weekend something strange happened. The boys all walked to the local diner together. They sat at the bar with root beer floats, laughing and joking usually at each other's expense. Jason looked at him self in the large mirror behind the bar. Behind him, he could see a man watching him. Every time Jason looked he noticed the man was staring. It made him feel uneasy. His senses picked up on it, making a tight knot in his stomach.

After the Root Beer float came the hot dogs and malted milk. Jason jumped down from his stool to use the rest room. As he got closer to the end of the diner, he could see his reflection in the highly polished chrome on the Jukebox. The man had got up and was following Jason. He felt uneasy, so he stopped and looked at the records on the Jukebox. The man passed behind him and went into the restroom. Jason decided he would wait and went back to join the others.

Fifteen minutes passed, and Jason attempted to go again. The same thing happened. The man watched him, got up, and followed him towards the restroom. It gave Jason the creeps so he gave up on the idea until he got back to the academy.

*

As he expected, Jason was by far the best in the karate class and was chosen to represent the Quentin Roosevelt Military Academy. It was the first time in the academies history that a first year student had ever been allowed to represent them, and he was told he would probably be the youngest and smallest in the games. He was allowed to choose three students who could also take the trip to US Marine Corps camp in California. He chose Tex, Yankee, and Cowboy; they were all thrilled to be going.

The students were packed in a cargo plane and flown the fifteen hundred miles to Camp Pendleton in California. They were housed in large tents with make shift beds. Jason was surprised how comfortable they were. He found the more time he spent in the United States with the military, the more he enjoyed it. The nickname 'Limey' still annoyed him, but he had to accept it and felt like part of the group.

The Games were set to start on Monday. In

all, over twenty-two military academies across America had sent representatives. They took it very seriously. They were given strict orders. Most of the time they had to observe and support various competitions. They could eat what they wanted in the various makeshift mess halls. The US Marines provided the food. Jason enjoyed it. He noticed various television news crews also attended some of the events.

Jason, Tex, Cowboy, and Yankee walked inside the perimeter of the base after dinner. They were in uniform and noticed they were getting a lot of stares from others. There were hundreds of contestants and supporters. They couldn't quite put their finger on what it was, but they were getting checked out by the others.

"What are they all staring at us for?" Tex asked.

"It's you and your red hair." Cowboy grinned.

"No it's you, Cowboy. They haven't seen many bow legged people." Jason smiled.

"No it's you, Limey, with your crazy blond hair and how you speak." Yankee laughed. "Bloody barbaric Americans, I say. What, no hot tea, just coffee?" He scoffed trying to sound like Jason.

They all laughed together but they stopped short when a group of five cadets approached them. The group all looked aged around fourteen to sixteen. It was getting dark, and Jason couldn't quite make out their academy on their uniform. The older cadets studied the younger boys. They looked at Tex. He recognized a few. One in particular was the lead cadet called Carver. Tex remembered him and that he was a bully.

Carver stepped forward. “Why, if it’s not Luttrell and his new Quentin Roosevelt Military Academy buddies. What are you doing here Luttrell? No way you're good enough to compete,” the youth said. Jason thought he sounded just like Tex.

"Oh hi guys. No, I'm just a spectator," Tex said. The older Cadets were all from Fort Worth Military Academy in Texas., It was where he spent his first year before graduation top of his class and being sent to Quentin Roosevelt Academy.

Carver sidestepped towards Yankee. “So, you get to have your own slave at your posh academy, Luttrell?” He sneered, looking at Yankee.

“Hey, come on guys. No need for that. He’s one of us. His skin color has nothing to do with anything,” Tex argued.

Carver spat on his boot. He turned and grinned to his four friends before looking back at Yankee. “Hey, boy. See that on my boot? Get down and wipe it off.”

Yankee gulped. He had heard rumors that some people in the south were living in the past and racist but had never witnessed it first hand before. Sweat beads started to break on his black brow; he was unsure what to do.

"Guys, he's one of us. He's cool. He's from New York. We call him Yankee." Tex stuttered.

"Luttrell, unless you want me to rub my boots on that red hair of yours, shut the hell up. I was talking to your boy here." He looked again at Yankee. "Listen boy, I told you to get down and wipe that off my boot."

Yankee paused. He took out a tissue from his pocket and knelt down to wipe his boot.

"Don't you dare, Yankee. You're wearing the uniform of the Quentin Roosevelt Military Academy. You don't have to do that," Cowboy said, stepping forward and facing Carver.

"I'm gonna have to teach you some manners, Pickaninny lover." Carver hissed, throwing his fist and catching Cowboy on the side of his face. Cowboy was knocked down by the blow. Carver stepped forward to kick him, but Jason caught his arm and held him back. Carver glared at Jason.

"Who the hell do you think you are touching blond?" Carver shouted.

Jason pushed Carver back. "That's enough. Let us pass we don't want any trouble," Jason said.

Carver and his fellow Cadets roared with laughter. "Luttrell, just who are you hanging with? a Pickaninny and an Australian with a death wish?"

Tex was unsure what to say. He and Yankee helped Cowboy off from the ground. Tex and the others knew Jason was best at the academy in karate, but had never seen him fight and doubted he could take on more than one or two. They were still out numbered.

"That's Limey. He's a Brit and representing our academy in the martial arts competition," Tex said. He looked at Jason, not sure if he should have said it or not. He was concerned it may make matter worse. The reply brought more laughter. Carver moved forward to Jason.

"So blue eyes, you know Kung Fu?" Carver said as he waved his arms around. Eventually he tried to slap Jason's face. Jason caught Carvers hand and twisted it, forcing Carver to fall to his knees.

"Let us pass, guys. We don't want any trouble," Jason pleaded. He released Carver, hoping he would back off.

Instead, Carver swung at Jason. This time Jason blocked it and returned a punch, catching Carvers face. Immediately, the other four older cadets attacked Jason. One threw a punch. It was a simple block. Another kicked at him, but Jason ducked and retaliated with a kick of his own, catching the youth in the stomach and sending him back several yards. Jason stepped back and took a breath. He looked at Tex, Cowboy, and Yankee.

"Come on, let's get back to our quarters," Jason said.

The four boys set off running as fast as they could but were chased by Carver and his fellow cadets. Tex ran between two buildings. The others followed, but it was blocked by the perimeter fence. They were trapped. Jason turned and noticed his pursuers had now increased in numbers. Three more from Fort Worth Academy had joined Carver and the others. Jason cursed; he looked at Tex, Yankee, and Cowboy.

"Stay back by the fence," Jason said. He turned and faced his followers and stood in a fighting stance. "I have to warn you. I know martial arts and will use it. Back off and leave us alone. I will defend myself." He was unsure of the law in the United States. He knew in Great Britain if he ever used martial arts he had to warn people first, else it would be considered use of a weapon. Where Jason was concerned, that weapon could be deadly.

Carver ran towards Jason followed by the others. He swung his fists widely at Jason. each attempted strike was blocked. When another cadet came close, Jason hopped on one leg, span around, and kicked out, catching Carver and the other Cadet one after another. Carver was knocked to the ground. Three other cadets moved in towards Jason.

One stood in a fighting stance and threw a roundhouse kick towards Jason. The youth obviously knew some karate and was sure he could take down the smaller boy. Jason blocked the kick, dropped to his hands in a push-up position, span around, and swept the boys legs away. He fell in a heap, and before he could recover, Jason pounced on his chest, landing on his knee. He threw two fast punches at the boy's face. The second blow shattered the boy's nose.

Carver scooped up a large handful of gravel and dirt, then he tried to kick Jason, knowing the boy would block it. However, when Jason did block, Carver threw the dirt into Jason's eyes. The grit immediately stung Jason's eyes. They streamed with tears, and he frantically tried to rub then clean. Carver took his chance and punched Jason. He caught him just above his right eye, and then another cadet moved in as well. Together, they started to pummel the smaller boy.

Jason was temporarily blinded. His eyes felt like they were on fire. Punch after punch caught his face as he desperately tried to wipe his eyes. He thought back to his training in Hong Kong and what his mentor, Wong Tong, had always taught him. Jason forced his eyes open and ignored the pain. Instinctively, he blocked the punches. He induced an adrenaline rush into his body. He caught a fist. Whose it was Jason did not know or care. He was now in self-defence mode. His pupils dilated black as he concentrated to make out the shapes around him. He caught and twisted a fist coming towards him with one hand and struck down with his other hand, breaking the boys wrist. It was Carver. and he screamed out in pain, falling to his knees as he held his wrist.

Jason's vision was blurred. He tried to make out the figures around him. As he kicked out at his attackers, he caught one cadet by the collar with his left hand and pulled him. As he did, his right fist catapulted from his body. Inches from impact, Jason threw his shoulder into the punch. The impact shattered three ribs. The injured youth went down like a trapdoor was opened beneath his feet. Jason leapt over the fallen cadet and Carver who was now sobbing on the ground holding his broken wrist. The cadet who had previously kicked Jason was now terrified. Jason elbowed the youth in the face, cracking his jaw and breaking three teeth.

It was now obvious that they needed to contain Jason. He was like a wild animal. His arms and legs shot out at his attackers. The more they tried to hurt him. The more they got hurt.

The commotion drew a large crowd. A Jeep pulled up and three military policemen jumped out, running towards the fight. They had no idea who was fighting who. They saw four cadets on the ground, some bleeding and some fighting. The first MP to arrive pulled two cadets back and threw the youths on the ground, trying to break up the fight. Jason had caught hold of a cadet and had him in an arm lock. He used his right leg to kick out at another attacker.

A second MP caught Jason's collar and pulled him off the youth. Jason retaliated and threw the MP over his shoulder, pounced on him and punched the MP four times in the face. The third MP tried to help his colleague. He attempted to grab Jason, but his hand was blocked. Jason sprung to his feet and kicked the MP to the ground. While the MP fell to his knees, Jason span around and smashed the side of his foot into the MP's face.

Cowboy ran towards Jason and shouted at him. “Jason stop! They’re MPs.” Jason sprung back to his feet and stood at an angle to Cowboy on his toes. He tried wiping his eyes to see clearer. Cowboy gingerly went towards him, “Don’t hit me, Jason. It’s me, come here.” Cowboy was a little nervous approaching him. He caught Jason’s arms and took him towards the side of a shed. He bent down and turned on a faucet. Jason knelt down and washed his head under the running water to clean the grit from his eyes.

A very large crowd had gathered. More MPs arrived along with three ambulances. Jason was taken to the military police station. He was shown into an interview room and locked in.

Chapter Twelve

The next six hours seemed like a bad dream. Jason was interviewed along with Cowboy, Tex, and Yankee. He knew he would be in trouble for fighting but never expected it to be as bad as it was. The list of injuries to the other cadets was long, but worse still were the injuries on the MPs. He was told that if he had been an adult serving in the armed forces he would be facing court martial and a prison sentence of three to five years. Because he was a cadet, he was still classified as a civilian and being only twelve they were uncertain what to do. It was very embarrassing for the MP's. They were trained to break up fights between US Marines, a cadet injured all these.

The games organizers met and discussed the situation. After four hours debate they finally announced their decision.

The entire Quentin Roosevelt Military Academy was banned from the 1975 games. The entire staff, all competitors, and Quentin Roosevelt supporters were to leave Pendleton within twenty-four hours. It would be the first time in over sixty years that the Quentin Roosevelt Military Academy would not be competing. Many of the cadets took the news badly. Generations of family members had attended the games, and now they had to explain that they had been banned for the year.

A few newspapers picked up on the story. The headline read *Quentin Roosevelt Military Academy Banned From Games*. The stories went on to say that it was due to a fight that broke out over racial comments. The whole story read like it was Jason's, Cowboy's, Tex's, and Yankee's fault. The bad news wasn't over yet eight. Everyone at the academy gave the four boys bad looks. Jason was to report to the commander on his return.

Jason marched into the commander's office. He saluted and removed his hat and took in his surroundings. The commander was sat behind a large rosewood desk. Behind him were a couple of big flags. There was the Stars and Stripes with a gold fringe and what he guessed was the South Dakota state flag.

Commander Gates studied the boy. He looked at Corporal Jones and pointed at Jason with his pipe. "This little thing is the boy who did all this?" He looked down at the mound of paperwork full of reports and complaints.

Corporal Jones swallowed. "Yes, sir. This is Private Steed."

"Private Steed, we have contacted the admiralty in England. They are just as disappointed in you as we are. Have you any idea how embarrassing this is for us? Did you see what you did, the amount of people you injured and put in hospital? Good god, boy, we're supposed to be on the same side. This has not helped Anglo-American relations like it was supposed to do. It's a damn shame I can't do more than just expel you and send you home. If I had my way—"

Jason interrupted him. "Expel me sir?" Jason was horrified. He finally found a school he loved and was to be expelled and sent home.

"Well, you can hardly stay on here, now can you?"

"What would you have done in my situation, Sir?" Jason asked, his eyes filled with tears.

Commander Gates looked at Jason and softened slightly. "Well..." He paused and exhaled. "I wouldn't have put three MPs in hospital."

"Sir, I couldn't see. They threw dirt in my eyes. They were calling Yankee racist names and wanted him to wipe spit off this bullies boot. It was Cowboy that stopped that, then he got hit for helping and was about to get kicked. I was just defending Cowboy and myself. Should I have let them kick Cowboy and let Yankee, a Quentin Roosevelt Military Academy cadet no less, wipe spit off another cadets boot just because of his skin color?" Jason stopped himself. He was brimming with emotion. The last thing he wanted to do was cry in front of the commander. He took a deep breath.

"Please sir, what *should* I have done?" he

asked again.

"Well ah..." The commander stuttered and placed his pipe in his mouth. "It's irrelevant now. What's done is done. Until I decide what to do, you will be confined to your room." He paused and looked at Corporal Jones. "His roommate can fetch his dinner. For now, he leaves him room just to use the bathroom. That will be all for now gentlemen."

*

QRMA's officers and training instructors put their heads together and decided that Jason and his group of friends needed a sharp reminder about the importance of discipline. The reminder would take the form of two-day hike across South Dakota's countryside, led by the notorious Corporal Armstrong. All QRMA instructors were tough, but Armstrong was the worst because he got a huge kick out of making students suffer.

All four boys were dropped off the back of a truck just before dawn and Armstrong gleefully announced that they each had to carry a twenty-five pound weight, on top of the tent, utensils, drinking water, and clothing already crammed inside their backpacks.

Despite all four boys being fit, they found the punishment hell. Armstrong, who drove in a Jeep, kept reminding them that a student could quit at anytime. They knew if they wanted to graduate they had to get through it. A ruthless instructor who didn't care if you're crying, injured, or sick pushed your body and brain to breaking point. All he cared about was toughening up the students so they could cope with all the bad stuff that might happen in the military. When it was punishment they made it extra hard.

The two-day course chosen would normally be tackled in three days. To do it in two they had to forgo sleep one of the nights. They arrived back at the academy two days later exhausted with blister-covered feet and hungry.

“Took you four men long enough to get back here. Jason, you're still confined to your room,” Armstrong ordered. The boys were tired, but being called men by Armstrong lifted their spirits. Jason stood in the shower, trying to refresh and refocus. It took a minute for the water to heat up, but as soon as it did, Jason wished he never had to leave. By the time Tex and the others had eaten and brought food back, he was in his bunk asleep.

For two more days Jason stayed in his room. He ventured out into the corridor only to use the bathroom or shower. He did go to the end of the corridor to use the phone to call Scott but never went through with the call. He didn’t think he could bring himself to say the actual words he was getting expelled from the academy. Just thinking about it and the shame it would bring to his father put him off the idea.

He was working out in the bedroom, push-ups, karate forms, and sit-ups when someone knocked at the door.

“Come in, it’s not locked.” Jason panted. He

was doing stretching exercises, his right leg was held straight up, with his knee almost touching his face. Jason looked as the door opened. A slim man with dark hair stepped in. Jason recognized him. *The weirdo from the dinner,* Jason said to himself he immediately lowered his leg and faced the man.

"I like girls," Jason said, although as soon as he'd said it he thought how stupid he must have sounded. The man looked at him and smiled.

"Good. But why is that relevant now?" The man grinned. Jason studied him, He was about thirty. He looked fit, with dark hair and large brown watchful eyes. Maybe even good-looking Jason thought.

"Cause you're a Willy watcher?" Jason said in way that sounded like a question.

"Ha ha. Whatever gave you that idea Jason?" The man laughed.

"You were watching me at the diner. Then when I went to use the bathroom you got up and followed. I never went in and waited. When I tried again you went in again. What were you hoping to see?"

"Oh, I see and you think that I wanted to..." He paused. "No, that was the furthest thing on my mind. If I made you feel uncomfortable, I'm sorry."

"You come any closer and I'll make you sorry," Jason said still not trusting the stranger.

"So you're the famous Jason Steed. Born March 24, 1963 in Hong Kong. Your mother was a Scottish champion athlete and an Olympic bronze medal winner. Your father is English and serves in the Royal Navy. An IRA bomb killed his parents just over a year before you were born. You're a third Dan black belt in Taekwondo, and you hold black belts in Judo and other forms, plus you've also studied Jiu Jitsu. You are the youngest person to receive the Queen's Award for Bravery and the Victoria Cross. And probably the youngest in Europe to hold a pilot's license. You have worked with various intelligence agencies on missions." He smiled at Jason and continued. "Plus, you are very close friends to the Queen's youngest daughter, Princess Catherine, and you have a vicious temper that you can't control. Shall I go on?"

"If you know so much about me, when did I last take a pee?" Jason asked.

The man laughed and extended his hand to Jason, who reluctantly shook it. "You're much smaller than I expected, Jason, but I guess you are only twelve. Let me introduce myself. I'm Max Fisher I work for D.O.D."

"D.O.D., what's that? Dumbasses On Drugs? What do you want?" Jason asked.

Max grinned at Jason's remark.

"That's a good one Jason, but it actually stands for Department of Defense."

"So, why do you know so much about me? I

told the general I was defending Cowboy and I didn't know it was the MPs I was hitting. They threw dirt in my eyes. I don't want to get expelled. You don't know what it's like not having a mum, a real family. My father is always away at sea. I love it here at the academy. Why does the dodos have to get involved? I really want to stay here."

"It's D.O.D., Jason, and this has nothing to do with the brawl you got into at Camp Pendleton, although that has caused enough problems. Didn't they tell you in Britain you would be contacted over here?"

"Yes but I thought by a..." Jason paused. "Em, No." Jason was unsure what to say. He assumed he would be making contact with British intelligence. He scratched his head and sat on his bunk.

"You make a terrible liar, Jason. Don't worry, my department works with the Brits and oversees most organizations here in the states, including the CIA. Jason, you are working for us. That's why you're here."

"No, I'm here to go to school and just keep an ear to the ground," Jason protested.

"And what would your father have said if we had asked if you could come in to the academy undercover?" Max asked. He sat next to Jason on the bunk.

"You're the smart one, you already know my dad would have said no."

"Exactly. So we came up with this, and it had the added benefit of bringing you to the world's top military academy where you could be among people more like yourself. Although you may have blown that with your fight at Pendleton, unless we can smooth it over."

Chapter Thirteen

Max Fisher spoke to Jason for almost three hours briefing him on the mission. He told him he had originally wanted to make contact at the diner and arrange a meeting, but Jason's paranoia spoilt that plan.

The United States government was working with a private company called Lockheed. They were building a new type of aircraft that could avoid enemy radar by a secret system called Echo 1. The aircraft would be built with flat panels that would be invisible to radar. The plane had the nickname of Stealth; the D.O.D was concerned that the details would get into the hands of the Russians or Chinese. They suspected a double agent was working and using the academy as cover.

Max would be working at the academy under cover as a new instructor teaching older students geography. The previous teacher became suddenly ill and left. They still needed Jason's help as Max would be suspected, as he was new. Max would let Jason do the snooping around and work with him on any information they could gather to find the suspected mole.

Jason agreed to help if it meant he could stay at the academy, although Max told him that was not going to be easy. They needed to find a suitable punishment that would keep everyone happy and not raise suspicions.

The General smoothed things over with Fort Worth Military Academy. They agreed to let him deal with Jason Steed and concurred that Carver had started the trouble Jason and his friends had just been defending themselves. Camp Pendleton was a different matter; the wounded MP's were embarrassed by the incident and exaggerated what Jason had done. Eventually they agreed to drop the matter as long as Jason Steed never returned to the games another year. He was banned for life.

Jason was allowed to return to his classes and confinement to his room was lifted. The dirty looks he was given by many of the students stopped after hearing what he had done to help Yankee and Cowboy.

Max Fisher kept his distance from Jason while he was in public, but would turn up at various locations to speak to Jason alone. In the library he spoke to Jason between the bookshelves. He crept into Jason and Tex's room one night to talk to him while both boys were sleeping. He woke Jason up and suggested they talk in the restroom.

"This had better be good. I was asleep, and I have a math test tomorrow." Jason yawned. He leaned back heavy against a row of sinks.

Max was his usual happy self. “I sometimes wonder if all what they say about you is true. So far you have given me nothing. You're just like a normal boy.” Max frowned.

“I *am* a normal boy. What did you expect, Sherlock Holmes? I’m just good at martial arts. I have no idea who the spy is. I’m new here I have seen nothing suspicious apart from you creeping around,” Jason argued. He yawned again, looked at his watch and his reflection in the mirror, and tightened the cord on his Pajamas. “It’s two in the morning. Can’t you find another time to chat to me?”

“Ah well actually, I have and you are going to enjoy it.” Max smiled. “Some of the special guard at the airbase heard about your karate skills. They train two times a week and they heard that you are over qualified for the academy martial arts class and agreed to let you join them training. It will be Mondays and Thursdays around six in the evening. You will be given a special pass.”

Jason came to life. He practiced a kick at himself in the mirror. “I'll be training with special forces? Whoa, bloody awesome. Will you want me to spy on them?”

“No, Jason. The airbase is secure. It’s the academy where we think we have the problem. Can you not think of anyone who is suspicious?” Max paused. “And don’t say me.”

Jason laughed. “No, I have no clue. I spend my time with my class. After class Tex, Yankee,

Cowboy, and me sometimes hang out. They're teaching me baseball, although it's just like a game I've played in England we call rounder's. Apart from that, I'm not sure what you want me to do. I never said I was a good spy."

"Well, keep an eye out. I'll get you your pass for Monday night. You will be the only one from the academy who has been given one to go into the airbase," Max said.

"Wait, maybe it's nothing but maybe it's something," Jason said.

"What?" Max said, gaining interest.

"Well, the night I arrived here, Corporal Jones said something strange."

"Corporal Jones? That guy's a idiot. He's far too stupid to be a spy for another country," Max said and continued. "Unless that's just a cover... What did he say?"

"He mentioned the Jakarta massacre. He knew I was involved."

"Well Jason, he probably just read your file," Max argued.

"No, he never knew it was me. He just knew it was a Sea Cadet, but he said, *one even escaped with a cassette we had that armed a nuclear warhead.*"

"I don't follow," Max said.

"Derr, I knew D.O.D stood for Dumbasses on

Drugs." Jason grinned. "A Cassette *we* had," he repeated. "What did he mean by *we*? Is he the agent working for the Chinese?"

"Wow Jason, that's impressive. Slow to give it to me since it happened when you arrived three weeks ago, but nevertheless something to go on. I will investigate him fully. Okay, you had better get back to bed. You have a math test tomorrow."

*

Three French sailors and four British naval personal taking part in the United Nations observation team, along with three journalists, were all arrested and imprisoned by the Vietnamese. The United Nations team members and journalists from Australia, Japan, and the United States were in coastal waters off Ho Chi Minh City in a small cruiser launched from British Aircraft Carrier HMS Hermes. The communist Vietnamese government accused them of spying because they came to shore to help with the relief work. The United Nations, along with the respective foreign governments, was trying to negotiate the release of the ten men.

*

Dressed in his karate gee, Jason proudly marched across from the Academy to the airbase. He showed his pass and was allowed into the base. The two-armed guards pointed him in the direction he needed to go. Two more armed guards greeted him and allowed him inside. Once inside, Alex Hannity, a well-built man with a shaved head, greeted him. Jason couldn't help but notice his tattoos that covered his arms and chest.

He spent the next two hours working out with the men. Much of it consisted with circuit training and various karate movements they called katas and finished off with non-contact sparing. Jason enjoyed sparing more than anything. He was of course much smaller and lighter than his opponents but made up for it with his incredibly fast reactions and moves. Often, they watched in astonishment at his moves. He switched from Taekwondo to Jiu Jitsu to Jeet Kune Do and, every now and then, he would throw an opponent in a Judo move.

On his way out, he passed several offices. They were closed the people working at the secret facility had gone home for the night. On one door he read the sign Radio Communications High Level Security. He tried the door to see just how secure it was and was surprised when it opened. After checking he was not being watched, he snuck inside and looked around. The room had large radios. They looked similar to his friends Scott's, but these were much larger and looked more modern. On the table, he noticed a folder marked Top Secret. Inside were codes for radio contacts. Jason had no idea what he could do with it but remembered Scott saying that the Americans used secret codes and could never understand what they were saying. *I bet Scott would love his. It'd make an awesome birthday gift*, he said to himself as he stuck it under his jacket.

He returned back to the academy covered in sweat. He had bruises on his forearms after blocking various blows. he couldn't wait to see Max again to thank him. He mailed out the secret codes to Scott the following morning, wishing he could see his friend's face when he opened it.

*

Tex and Jason joined Cowboy and Yankee for breakfast the next morning. It was the usual mocking of each other's accents, talking about girls, and what revolver would be best suited to carry. Jason felt strangely at home. He never missed his old school. Maybe Scott, but other than that, he was thoroughly happy.

Even more so, he enjoyed first lesson of the day—military training. Each week at the same time they were taught something of military importance and often had a guest speaker. Jason was delighted when Alex Hannity greeted the boys.

The three-hour lesson was jungle survival training. Hannity had returned from Vietnam just five months earlier. He had spent six years fighting in 'Nam as he called it. He had lost many friends and colleagues during the war. He called the North Vietnamese the Vietcong, and he recalled events to the enthusiastic youngsters in Jason's class. He covered how to survive by eating certain bugs and snakes as well as what plants to eat and avoid. He was awarded the Purple Heart. In a question and answer session at the end of the lesson, Yankee asked him what he hated the most about the war. He replied coming home to America. He was walking down a street and called a baby killer and literally spat on.

It was shocking to hear how he and many were treated. However, reports had hit the news that some troops had raped Vietnamese woman. Over four hundred thousand civilians had been caught up in the cross fire from both sides. Alex Hannity had to take a breath at one moment to prevent himself from breaking down. He explained that, in all wars, bad things happen. Your job, as a solider, is to follow orders on behalf of your country.

The whole class enjoyed the lesson and was disappointed when the bell went for lunch break. They all saluted him and thanked him for his service as they left.

Chapter Fourteen

Jason was called into the commander's office just after lunch. He suspected it had something to do with the fight at Camp Pendleton. He'd hoped by now they would drop the matter and let him get on with his studies. He knocked at the door and was told to wait.

He was concerned about seeing the commander. He would rather face a group of samurai assassins. He knew how to handle them. The commander, on the other hand, was far more unpredictable.

"Come in," the commander called. Jason marched in and saluted. The commander swiftly saluted back and sucked on his cigar and the tip glowed an angry red. "Ah Jason, please take a seat. I need to talk to you."

"Yes, Sir. Thank you, Sir," Jason said. He was now worried. The commander never called anyone by his or her first name.

"Jason, have you been watching the news?"

"Em. Not really. I don't really understand

American football yet to follow it." Jason paused when he noticed the commander frown. "That's not what you meant is it, Sir?"

"No, Jason. I meant international news matters, such as the Russian spaceship and the US Apollo linking up in space or the situation in Vietnam," the commander asked, closely watching the boy. Jason shrugged. "Did you know the British ship HMS Hermes is off the Vietnam waters?"

"Yes, Sir. I mean, no, Sir. I didn't know where it was but I know the Hermes. That's my father's ship. He's the ship's Second Lieutenant. Sir." Jason paused. He noticed the commander shift awkwardly in his seat and pretend to re-light his pipe. "Is my Dad okay?" Jason's voice fell off.

"Yes is the straight forward answer. The North Vietnamese have taken him and nine other men prisoner. He was working for the United Nations on a small cruiser, mostly monitoring events. He and three other British naval personnel where taken along with three French personnel and three journalists."

Jason got up and paced up and down trying to think. "Where is he? Is he safe? Why is he a prisoner? The British aren't at war with the Vietcong. What is the Admiralty doing to release him?"

"Jason, I don't know the answers. The American government is also working on it. One of the journalists is American. The Vietnamese have not yet given any demands. They have just accused them of spying."

"He's in the Royal Navy. What was he doing working for the United Nations?" Jason asked.

"The United Nations is an organization made up from representatives from armed forces around the world. I suspect he and others were instructed to work alongside the French and any other country to help. They do a lot of good. They're peacekeepers. Never before in its twenty-year history has anyone working as a United Nations representative been held before. The world community strongly condemns such action."

"Thank you for the information, Sir," Jason said stiffly before clicking his boot heels and leaving the room feeling sick to his stomach. He was worried. Alex Hannity and others had told them about the Vietcong prisons. They had witnessed some of the American POW's return to the airbase. Many looked emaciated, too weak to walk more than a few paces. Tex and Jason thought one looked too old to be a prisoner of war. The man looked about sixty. They later found out he was only aged twenty-nine but was held in a Vietnamese prison for three years.

Tex heard the news and skipped the last lesson to find Jason. He found him in the gym attacking a boxing punch bag. Jason was stripped to the waist. He had taken off his shoes and socks and was kicking and punching the bag for all he was worth. Jason's knuckles had split open. The bag had his blood on the front of it where he had been pounding it.

"Wow, Limey I think you killed him," Tex joked. Jason paused and looked at his knuckles. He threw one last punch at the bag. "Come on man, let's go and get your hands seen to. I heard about your father. I'm sure he'll be okay if he's as tough as you."

Jason nodded and followed Tex who took him to the sick bay where the nurse treated his hands. The next twenty-four hours passed like a blur to Jason. He wasn't given any more news. He watched the TV, hoping to get some news but nothing new was reported. Out of options, he decided to call his father's Uncle Stewart.

"Steed residence," Stewart Steed answered.

"Uncle Stewart, it's Jason."

"Jason dear boy. My favourite second nephew."

"I'm your only second nephew."

"I was just thinking about you. I expect you heard the news. Don't worry ,your father is a Steed. We're a tough family."

"I can't find out anything. He's been a prisoner for two days now. Why isn't the British Government sending in troops to rescue them? The Hermes is right there."

"It's not that simple, son. The United Nations is dealing with it. They are negotiating, but the demands are too high."

"What demands? Dad and the others were just observing, making sure the civilians didn't get massacred."

"The Vietnamese have made demands. I don't know what they are, but the Prime Minister said they are unacceptable. The French President has said the same thing. For now, the international community has condemned the Vietnamese, but nothing has been done yet. Son, there is nothing you can do. Please try to relax. Your father will be just fine. You concentrate on showing those Yankees a thing or two on how to be a good cadet."

Jason felt a little better after talking to Uncle Stewart. He was not close to him and found him stuck up, but at a time when he needed to talk to someone he was there. There was something else about him Jason found harder to place. A certain guarded quality in his voice, a sense of tension. Jason had a terrible thought. If his father was killed, whom would he have to live with? It would be a choice between his uncle and his mother's parents in Scotland. He thought about it and thought his grandparents in Scotland would be better, and then he cursed at himself for thinking about his father dying.

*

Jason discovered he had gained an unwanted celebrity status at the academy. All the students and teachers alike spoke about the first year boy from Britain whose father was one of the prisoners. At almost every class the teacher would ask him how he was holding up. A television news crew had heard the story that one of the British officers held prisoner had a son who was a student at the academy. They were denied access, but ran a story from outside the gates anyway, although they never knew the name of the student or his father.

A week flashed by. The allied governments refused to give into demands from the Vietnamese. The United Nations tried in vain to keep talks going and free the ten men. The Vietnamese knew the Americans would not step foot on Vietnam again. They had seen the news reports of Americans marching on the streets demanding an end to the war. Now it was ended, America was not in the mood to start all over again with Vietnam. The French were in the same situation; they had been at war with Vietnam in the early 1960s and did not want a repeat. The British were more bullish, but after seeing the Americans fail knew they would never get support from the public to launch an assault. The only thing left was a diplomatic solution.

Jason was in the common room after dinner with around twenty other boys watching the news. A news headline was announced half way through the scheduled news program. The Vietnamese had announced that unless the foreign governments agreed to their demands they would start executing the prisoners. They gave ten days. After that deadline, one prisoner would be shot every day.

All eyes in the room fell on Jason. He sat staring at the TV not sure how to react. He felt like crying, but felt sick at the same time and then angry, very angry. He left the common room to use the phone. He called George Young at his home a woman answered the phone.

"This had better be good. It's two in the morning," A woman's voice answered.

"Hello Jean, its Jason. Sorry if I woke you." Jean Young knew Jason well; they had spent time together in Spain with George and Jean's son, Martin. Jason had saved both Jean and Martin's life.

"Jason. Hello pet, I'm so sorry to hear about your father. I'm sure they will get him out safely."

"Thanks Jean. I need to speak to George," Jason said. George had followed his wife down the stairs he suspected the call was for him anyway.

"Jason son, how the bloody hell are you?" George asked.

"Not good George. What are they doing about getting my dad out? It's just been on the news that in ten days they are going to start executing them." Jason felt his voice shaking. He fought off his tears.

George sighed. "I know, son. They're doing everything they can. I'm sure it won't come to that."

"What are the demands what do they want?" Jason cursed.

"I don't know, son—" Before he could continue, Jason interrupted.

"Find out. I need to know, George. My dad has lots of money. If they want that they can have it."

"It won't be money. Besides, if it was you can bet it would be millions, and the British Government would erm, well maybe not."

"Would not what?"

"Well, we don't give into demands to kidnappers for money, else every bloody tourist would get kidnapped for money. I'll try and find out."

"Don't try, George. *Find out*. You're the head of SYUI; you know the top people in the admiralty, MI6, MI5. I will call tomorrow. Please try and find out." Jason hung up and called Scott. It was six rings before it was answered.

He first spoke to Scott's father, Doctor Turner, before Scott came to the phone.

"Jase mate. How are you?" Scott asked.

"Not good. Did you hear what's happening with my dad?" Jason said. "Oh your voice has broken. You sound cool."

"Yeah, so do you. I heard about your dad and the new deadlines/ I'm sure it won't come to that."

"What do you expect me to do, just sit around and wait and do nothing?"

"Well, there isn't much you can do." Scott

paused. "You do know that not even you can help him."

"I'll call Catherine's Mum, maybe she can help."

"If she could have she would have. She may be the queen, but even she can't interfere with foreign governments."

"This is bull. I thought you were my best friend!" Jason screamed and slammed down the phone. He walked back to his room with a large black cloud over him. After five minutes he went back to the phone and called Scott back. This time it was picked up on the first ring.

"Apology accepted," Scott answered without being prompted.

"Yeah, sorry mate. I feel so helpless," Jason said. They spoke for another fifteen minutes. He felt better for calling him back but after talking to everyone he never got any further. When he returned to his room, Tex was already in his bunk asleep. Jason climbed into his bed and lay with his eyes open, looking at the ceiling. His mind was racing, he was not in the slightest bit sleepy. It would take him another five hours before he eventually fell asleep.

Chapter Fifteen

It was Saturday. Although the students had no schoolwork, they did have assault course training in the morning. Jason sat it out. He went into the town center and bought every newspaper he could. He was desperate for news. He glanced at each paper, trying to find new information. His eyes darted across the pages, searching for some hope. He ran back to the academy and watched the TV news. It mentioned in a small segment noting that the prisoners had only nine days left before the threatened executions started.

He called George Young again. George had heard that the Vietnamese government wanted the trade sanctions imposed on them by the US lifted. In addition, they ere demanding compensation for the losses caused by the war and an apology from the United States President. Jason knew that would never happen. George tried to reassure him that the United Nations would win the Vietnamese over with talks, but Jason wasn't so confident.

George had heard that the ten prisoners were being held at a secret prison camp near Tay Ninh. The name meant nothing to Jason, but at least it was the name of the place where his father was being held. He dressed in his karate gee and used his pass to get into the air base. The guards assumed he was going to practice karate with some of the security staff again.

Once inside the airbase, Jason made his way to the storage hangers. They were full of used supplies that had been brought back from the Vietnam War—uniforms, weapons, and even some Jeeps. He searched through wooden trunks and footlockers; he was delighted when he came across combat knives, guns, belts, helmets, grenades, maps, and compasses. He collected some maps and hid them under his Jacket.

Back in his room, Jason went through the collection of maps. Tex walked back in and startled him. Jason nodded and carried on looking at the maps. Tex joined him and eventually asked. "What are you looking for Limey? Where they're holding your father?"

"I just want to see where the prison camp is. It makes me feel closer to him," Jason said without looking up. He continued to look over the maps. He made notes on a small notebook. Tex thought it was a little weird and left him to his maps and his notes.

Jason put his boots and some clothing in a backpack. He made up a story and told Tex he was going back to the airbase for more karate training. Tex had no reason to doubt him, although Jason did feel guilty for lying to him. In a hanger he changed into his camouflage uniform. He packed some M67 grenades, a combat knife, maps, a compass, a flask, and water purification tablets. He picked up a M1911 pistol. It felt cold in his hand. The safety was on and it was loaded. He packed it in his belt with two full clips on ammunition.

The equipment was mostly used. Some even had a little mud and dirt it. The M1911 had some rust, but he hoped he would not have to use it. He wondered who had previously used it and if anyone had been injured or even killed by it.

He crept outside the hanger and waited to make his move. Darkness had spread across the airbase. There was partial light from the moon as it shone its beam across the airfield, casting great shadows. Jason felt alert. He had no real plan, he just knew he had to try and do something, and anything was better than nothing.

*

Raymond Steed peered through the rusted bars; he squeezed the front of his face through, trying to gasp some breaths of fresh air. The air in the prison cell was putrid, a mix of stagnant body odour, urine, and excrement. The ten men were only given a bottle of water and partly rotted mangos for the last two days. They were not given clean clothing, bedding. or even a toilet; they used a corner of the cell. One of the French naval officers had managed to find a small stick so they could push the excrement away from the square cell. It meant they didn't have to stand in it.

Ray pulled on the bars in anger; he believed

that the British would be coming at any moment to rescue them. He was the highest-ranking officer and tried to put on a brave face for the sake of the others, but deep down inside, he was as depressed as they were. The cell was too small for the ten men. When they all tried to sleep, there was barely enough room for all ten to lie down.

The make shift squalid prison was three miles east of Tay Ninh; it was a low-lying area of swampland. The ten strong United Nations team had no idea of their location. They were flown in by helicopter and dropped off. After a three-mile hike under gunpoint, they arrived at the prison. The American journalist, Carl Bradley, nicknamed it Costa Del Pig Sty. His humour helped keep the men amused.

The prison had been closed two years ago while the war was still raging due to its close location to the Americans. It was now over grown with vegetation. It was a perfect secret location for the Vietcong to keep the prisoners.

The Vietnamese Communist Party leader, Le Duan, knew all too well that the demands he put in place for the ten captives would never get met. His objective was to inflict pain on the Western governments and teach them a lesson for interfering in the Vietnamese civil war.

Le Duan had placed the Vietnam War veteran, General Chow, in charge of the prisoners. Chow was a ruthless Vietcong officer. During the war, he had been head of two prison camps in his region. Some of the US prisoners were subjected to the most barbaric tortures known to mankind.

US President Ford and British Prime Minister Harold Wilson were deeply concerned but felt hopeless and knew the fate of the ten captives. When they heard that General Chow was in charge of the prisoners, they feared the worse. Stories were still surfacing from Americans who were tortured, starved to death, and killed if they would not denounce the United States.

*

Jason watched the ground crew fuel the aircraft. The four-man crew gathered in an office sharing jokes. He noticed the C-9B Skytrain's side cargo door was still open. He made his move. He ducked down and raced across the airfield to the aircraft, leapt up inside, and looked for a suitable hiding place. There weren't many places to hide. It wasn't like a commercial aircraft. It had just five rows of seats. The rest of the plane was open and used for cargo. Above the five rows of seats he noticed overhead lockers. He found one stuffed with blankets. He took some out to make room and hid them under a seat, then he climbed up and closed the door after checking he would be able to open it himself.

An hour later the aircraft took off. It was cramped and he thought the aircraft was quite cold. He was glad he had chosen a locker with blankets.

The aircraft was empty. Its mission was to fly to Pearl Harbor in Hawaii. There it would refuel, the pilots would change, and it would then fly to U-Tapao Pattaya International Airport in Thailand. On arrival in Thailand, it would be loaded with used military equipment left over from the war and flown back to the US.

Jason stayed where he was for the entire nineteen-hour flight. He had two bottles of water with him and some beef jerky. After drinking the water one of the empty bottles came in handy when he needed it. His legs were painful towards the end of the flight. He desperately wanted to stretch them. He ignored the pain and thought of his father. If his calculations were correct, they now had just six days left before the deadline.

While the aircraft was landing in Thailand, he wondered what would be happening at the academy when Tex reported him missing. He was also unsure if an agreement had been made by the United Nations and Vietnam. Maybe his father had been released.

The crew left the aircraft and headed straight for the mess hall for some food and drinks. Slowly, Jason crept out of his hiding place. He found it painful to stand. His legs had been cramped for such a long time. The next thing he noticed was the humidity. The doors were still open on the aircraft. He found himself starting to sweat instantly.

It was dark on the airfield and raining heavily. Jason took advantage of it and ran from the plane with his backpack. He stopped at the side of a large hanger and tried to take in his surroundings. To his left was a larger well-lit area. It looked like the main airport. He assumed he was in the military section of the airport. US Army Jeeps, M35 Trucks ,and crate upon crate of weapons and other material were stored next to the hanger. In just a few minutes he was soaked through. The rain was warm and heavy. He now knew why the maps where all covered in plastic.

Chapter Sixteen

Jason noticed a solitary guard in a US army uniform was sheltering from the rain in a small wooden guard hut. The glow of his cigarette gave his position away. Jason checked his gun, tucked it in the back of his pants, and coolly walked towards the man. It wasn't long before the guard positioned his rifle in Jason's direction.

"Who goes there? This is a restricted area," the guard shouted. He then repeated it in Vietnamese. Jason was impressed the guard could speak it. Unable to speak Vietnamese, Jason replied in Chinese.

"I don't speak Thai, just English and Vietnamese," the guard said, thinking Jason was talking Thai. Jason kept walking forward. He knew Thai and Chinese were similar. He had no idea how to speak Vietnamese. They used an alphabet system, something completely different to Chinese.

"It's okay, I can also speak English," Jason said.

"You sound Australian or is it English?" The guard loomed up next to him, looking at him with unbelieving eyes. "What are you doing out here? You're soaked. Is your father in the Air Force? You've a US cadet uniform on."

Jason shook the guard's hand. He found it strange how people always trusted children. He knew that's why George Young had always used him for missions. No one would suspect a sweet looking, blond haired, blue-eyed boy was about to do what Jason had in mind.

"Want some gum?" The guard placed his rifle against the wall and dug in his pocket and pulled out some gum. Jason leapt on one leg twisted on his hips and threw a roundhouse kick at the guard, sending him sprawling on the ground in the corner. By the time he turned and looked up, Jason had his revolver pointing at him.

"I don't want to hurt you, so just do as I ask," Jason ordered.

The guard coughed and rubbed his wounded stomach. "You already hurt me. You don't look like a Charlie."

Jason had heard others at the academy mention the name Charlie. It was the nickname they gave to the Vietcong. From what he had heard, they used the word Victor Charlie on the radio for the letters VC or Vietcong. Later it was shortened to just Charlie. "That's because I'm not a Charlie. Did you hear about the ten prisoners being held captive?"

The guard tried to stand, but Jason waved the pistol in his face. "Yes of course I have," he replied. "They have about six days left. I doubt President Ford will dare get involved. Why?"

"Where are they being held?" Jason asked.

"I don't know son. I'm just a guard. Somewhere in 'Nam."

Jason walked towards the guard. He ordered him not to move. He placed his hand on the guards shoulder, dug his fingers into his neck, and squeezed his carotid artery. The guard groaned in pain and struggled; within moments he passed out.

Jason snuck around the airport and soon found something he could use, a Cessna single engine propeller plane. He had never actually flown one but had seen them at the English airport. He had trained at and heard how easy they were to fly. He spent fifteen minutes checking fuel, oil, and flaps. Once his flight check was complete, he removed the tail tie down.

He studied his maps. They were of no real use until he was over Vietnam. He planned to fly south for two miles. That would bring him to the coast. He would then follow the coastline east along the Gulf of Thailand; he marked his course on the map. He wanted to wait until first light but he was forced into action. The guard had regained consciousness and sounded the alarm.

With no time to spare, Jason started the engine. He grinned when it roared into life. Placing his backpack on his seat gave him the extra height he needed to see out the cockpit. He noticed a US

Army Jeep heading in his direction. Like any pilot, he would have liked to warm the engine and hold it on the brakes for a while. However, he had to move. He released the brakes and the little plane lurched forward. The Jeep was getting closer. Jason's path was blocked. He wouldn't be able to make it to the main runway. He opened the throttles and it shot forward.

The Jeep contained two US army soldiers; they caught up and kept with Jason as he sped across at an angle to the runway. One guard gestured with his rifle to stop. They pointed a spot lamp into the cockpit. Jason looked at the guard and smiled, making sure the guard got a good look at him. He said something to his colleague; he could clearly see it was a boy in the aircraft. They seemed unsure what to do. Before they could decide, the choice was made for them. The plane was moving too fast to get in front of now and getting close to the perimeter fence.

Jason applied full throttle. The engine spluttered, but after he adjusted the choke it carried on, with enough speed. Jason pulled back on the tiller, and the tiny plane roared up into the night sky. The plane's wings clutched the air, pulling the plane up and just missing the top of the fence by a few feet.

That was too close, Jason said to himself. His pulse pounded.

In a few minutes, the flying thief broke free of the clouds. Using the compass, he flew south. He was concerned with the height he flew at. He needed to navigate with the coastline. Too high and he wouldn't be able to see it, too low and he could hit a tree or power line. It took just a few minutes to reach the coast. The moonlight reflected off the water. There to the right was the beach. The pale sand caught his eye.

Relax and concentrate, he told himself. Jason turned east and followed the thin line of white water breaking on the shoreline below.

*

News of the aircraft's theft was picked up by US military intelligence and the CIA. The guard who was attacked was debriefed. He explained who his attacker was. His story was hard to believe until the security guards who had chased the aircraft in the Jeep also said they witnessed a boy at the aircraft's controls. News spread back to the United States and Department of Defence. Max Fisher had spent the last nine hours organizing a search party for Jason. When he heard the news, he almost didn't want to believe it, but the witness accounts matched Jason's description.

They added it all up and realized Jason must have snuck on board a plane and made his way to Thailand. Max Fisher called his superior; at first, he found the story hard to believe and asked to read the report on the boy. It wasn't long before they knew everything about him. Fisher put in a call to George Young. When he explained what happened George laughed.

"Welcome to my world, Mr. Fisher. That boy isn't easy to control. I heard he got into a dust up with some of your MPs." George laughed again.

"Yes, put some in the hospital, but that's irrelevant now. Do you think he may actually try and reach Vietnam and attempt to rescue his father? It's a suicide mission. This is pretty real. They will blow him out of the sky, and if he lands and gets caught, the poor boy will never be seen again," Fisher warned.

"Of course he will try. From what you said, he already made it to Thailand and stolen a plane. He did the same thing here, stole a plane in Spain and flew to France while being chased by the Triads. But don't worry too much about Jason Steed. If they catch him, it will be them who are never seen of again. I've seen him in action. Vicious little blighter he can be, and he's got a temper that even he can't control," George said. "His karate instructor, a Chinese guy Jason calls Wong Tong, taught him an old Chinese fighting technique of inducing an adrenaline rush into his system. It makes him faster, more alert, and bloody deadly. On top of his karate skills, he's very fast. He knows some of the most lethal of moves in martial arts. He's studied so many types. He's a great agent to have working for us. He has just two shortfalls."

"What are his shortfalls?" Max asked.

"His temper. When he loses it, he can go too far. Now that he's getting older and becoming a young teen, it's getting worse. The other is... well, he's just a kid. He's twelve and so of course he thinks like a kid. He's a great agent as no one would ever suspect a cute blond-haired, blue-eyed boy but you have to make an allowance that he's also just a kid. Good luck." George laughed.

"Mr. Young, this is no laughing matter. We need to stop him. It could spark off a major international incident."

"Like I said, welcome to my world. He's probably already in Vietnam. You won't hear anything until either he returns the hero or half the bloody country is blown up. Sorry to be so blunt. but that's Jason. What you get is what you see."

Max thanked him, although was no further forward. He was surprised by George's remarks. It was exactly the same as the reports he read on him. However, after meeting Jason, Max liked him. He was a nice, good-looking boy who seemed pretty harmless.

*

Jason followed the coast, eventually leaving Cambodia, and followed the Vietnamese coastline. He was concentrating, looking down following the coastline when the air shook and the blast of a Vietnamese Mig-21 Jet flew passed him. It made Jason jump. He watched it disappear in front of him, ark in the sky, and return. Jason turned his aircraft to lower his altitude. He wasn't very experienced at flying. He had done enough hours to get his license and flown a few times since. He knew he could not out run the Mig with its jet-powered engine. He was also lacking experience. Without a working radio, he couldn't talk his way out of it, so he carried on, descending the aircraft.

As he descended to the shoreline, he searched to find a landing site. At night, with just the moon, it would be very difficult and dangerous, but he had no option. He could barely make out the beach and what looked like a long, sandy shoreline. The Mig passed him again but this time fired some warning shots. Jason took it down, hoping the beach had no rocks, fences, or debris.

This is your captain speaking; the flight may get a little bumpy, Jason said to himself as he lowered the Cessna down as gentle as he could. The ground was a couple feet lower than he expected. As he lowered, he pushed forward on the tiller and hit a mound of sand. The plane bounced up again. He fought with the controls as sand was thrown into the air. He pushed forward on the tiller again. The plane continued to bounce and speed along the beach. He thrust the engine into reverse and opened the flaps. It veered to the right and shuddered to a halt as it sunk into the soft, wet sand.

He climbed out of the plane and landed in a foot of water. As he made his way up the beach, he could hear a helicopter approaching. He ran into the undergrowth until he was well hidden under a large canopy of trees, shrubs, and palm trees. The helicopter searched the area and found nothing but footprints. By the time troops arrived at the scene, Jason was gone.

Chapter Seventeen

As dawn broke, the area commander, General Chow, walked over to the prisoners. He was a short man with a patch over his left eye. Rumours were that he lost his eye after becoming unconscious when his helicopter crashed. Three days later, rescuers found him. A rat had eaten his eye and part of his cheek. General Chow kicked the bars on the cell door, drinking a mug of coffee. “One sugar or two?” General Chow laughed, slurping his brew.

Jean-Perr, a French sailor, stood and stepped towards the cell door. “Ta Gueule,” he shouted and shook the cell door. General Chow pulled out his revolver and pointed it at him. Defiantly, the Frenchman stood his ground and spat at Chow. In a moment he was dead. The bullet pierced his heart and exited through his back. hitting the wall and narrowly missing Ray Steed's head.

Three guards ran towards the prisoners hut with rifles pointed at the prisoners. Chow laughed and warned the prisoners the same would happen to them if they disrespected him. He adjusted his eye patch with his revolver before slipping it back into his holster and walking along the bamboo walkway.

He told some of the guards what a wonderful morning it was.

The Vietnamese would later issue a press release that Jean-Perr was shot while trying to escape. The press release also mentioned the prisoners now only had five days to live unless the demands were met.

*

An emergency conference call was set up with United States President Ford, British Prime Minster Harold Wilson, and French President d'Estaing. Also on the call was the head of intelligence and security from each country. After the preliminarily introductions and niceties, the meeting started. It was agreed that no action could be taken.

President Ford told d'Estaing that he was sorry for his country's loss and doubted Jean-Perr was actually trying to escape. He carried on and said a military strike was out of the question. The others all agreed. They had to hope and pray that the United Nation negotiators could persuade the Vietnamese to release the nine remaining prisoners.

Prime Minister Harold Wilson was not happy with the situation. He had four British men held that he felt responsible for. He suggested sending in the SAS. The French and US Presidents both disagreed. It would be seen as an act of war, and if the British SAS were captured, what next? Did they want to follow the French and Americans lead and have a failed war with the Vietnamese? Wilson reluctantly agreed. The men agreed to discuss the matter again in four days time, just twenty-four hours before the deadline.

*

Jason walked for no more than a mile until he came across the outskirts of a town. A sign named it Ha Tien. It was early morning. People were up and travelling to work on cycles or on foot. Some travelled in a small buggy pulled by an ox. They stared at Jason. He felt conspicuous. His blond hair and US Amy camouflage uniform didn't exactly blend in. He turned off the dirt road and went in among some older run down homes. Jason thought they looked like huts since they were mostly made of wooden sticks with grass roofs. He noticed a woman outside her home feeding some chickens in a cage. He approached her.

She looked at him and looked away. Jason took a dollar bill out of his pocket and waved it at her. She looked and laughed at him. He was unsure what she was saying but clearly had the wrong idea. He pointed at his clothing and hers and waved the money again. The woman laughed again. She became hysterical.

Jason took off his jacket and passed it to the woman. She seemed to understand what he wanted and bowed as if apologizing. She went into her home and came out with a cream coloured shirt and brown pants with a hole in the knee. Jason quickly took his off and dressed in them. He kept his pants on and put hers on over the top of his.

“Thank you,” he said. “Why else did you think I was offering you money?” Then it struck him. He felt embarrassed she had probably been around when the US troops had been there. He guessed why they would offer a woman money.

Jason pointed at a straw Vietnamese hat. She picked it up and held out her hand. He passed her another dollar. He thanked her and made his way back to the main road. Immediately, he felt less conspicuous. No one gave him a second glance. He came across a small market. It was nothing more than six or seven make shift stalls. People sold meat, fruit, and clothing. One man was trying to sell old US Army uniforms, hats, and even guns. Jason guessed the man had either stolen them or found them after the US troops pulled out.

As he passed the stall selling meat, he had to take a second look. It was selling what at first he thought was a small pig or even a sheep, but when he looked closer, this thing had canines. It was a skinned dog. The stallholder was cutting another one up, and a woman was buying parts of it. Jason made a mental note not to eat any meat while he was in Vietnam. He studied his map and headed Northeast, He hadn’t travelled very far when he came across a disturbing scene.

A group of six boys around fourteen were beating two younger boys around ten. Jason watched for a while, not sure if he should intervene or not. Eventually, he moved closer. The boys getting beaten looked different but he couldn’t quite put his finger on it.

"Stop it, that's enough," he said and repeated it in Chinese, although he doubted they would understand either. They looked at him and surrounded him. One-stepped forward and attempted to hit him. He caught the boys hand sand twisted it. Another came forward, and Jason threw out a kick at the youth, catching him in his stomach. He released the first youth and shouted at them again. They looked at him bewildered and called him a name. "Con lai." Jason never understood what the word meant, but they all started chanting it.

A woman stepped forward with a broom and shouted at the youths, waving it madly at them. They ran off still chanting the word "con lai." She nodded at Jason and started to walk away. The two smaller children followed her, looking back at Jason and smiling at him with thanks.

"Thank you," he said to her, brushing himself off. She turned and looked at him and looked around nervously to make sure no one else was watching.

"You speak English?" she asked.

Jason smiled at her. He guessed she was one of the children's mothers. "Yes Ma'am. I'm glad I found someone else who can." Jason smiled.

She beckoned Jason to follow her and the children to a nearby home. Jason was stunned by how bare it was inside, containing only a large mattress on the floor, some blankets, a few wooden boxes, chairs, a table, and an oil lamp.

"You're not from around here. You must be careful. Many people in this village despise children like you, my son, or his friend. Your sort are not welcomed by many," she said.

Jason looked at the two boys, he was trying to work out which one was her son. They looked different to him. One had dark skin, almost black, but had the eyes of an Asian. The other looked like a westerner, even had red hair, but had the eyes of an Asian.

"Our sort?" Jason asked.

"Yes, you know Amerasian or "con lai" as they called you."

"Ameri what an? And what does *con lai* mean in English?" Jason asked. The darker coloured boy passed Jason a cup of water. "Thanks."

"Con lai means half breed. Your father was an American and so was these boys' fathers. My son is called Yung, but his father called him Ian. Yung's father was killed six years ago when Yung was just three. This is Keong. His mother was forced by an American soldier or so she says. He has never met his father. The correct term is Amerasian"

Jason drunk the water and took it all in. "So you married an American?"

"We were in love." She beamed. "We never married, although we planned to when the war ended. He was stationed here during the war. You must have seen other Amerasians? There are many of your kind here."

"Em." Jason paused and thought this could be the perfect cover for him. "Yeah I have. So doesn't your boyfriends parent's help out or the US government? Yung's father was an American; he would have had a benefit paid out or something to his son or you. Don't the Amerasians get anything from the United States?"

"No, they deny Yung's existence. His father wrote to his parents in America and told them about our son, but they would never accept him as a grandson. My family cast us out. They call me a whore. Yung's father was called Derek," she said, passing a picture of him to Jason. The picture was faded and creased. "He taught me to speak English. Did *your* mother teach you?"

Jason studied the picture. "Yes she did," he lied. "My mother is ill. I need to contact her family in Tay Ninh."

"That's too far for you to travel. It's about one hundred miles away. How were you planning to get there?"

"I don't know, walk." Jason shrugged.

"It will take you days, and you being Amerasian will have more trouble on the way. I'm afraid for many people you represent a depressing time for us in Vietnam. They will blame you for the loss of their loved ones."

Jason sat back and rested his head against

the stick wall. He felt tired. He hadn't slept and was overcome with jet lag. He woke up with a start some seven hours later. He was annoyed at himself for falling asleep. It was just after three in the afternoon. He had wasted valuable daylight hours. He said his goodbyes and left the small family.

After walking just a few miles he started feeling tired. The humidity was saturating and sapped his strength. He found himself on a dusty road. He passed burnt out and rusted tanks, Jeeps, and US Army troop carriers. He stopped and rested in a rusted army truck. The door squealed as he pulled it open to rest inside. He took advantage of his break to look at his map. Using his compass he could work out where he was. He was walking almost parallel with the Cambodian border.

The route he had taken brought him to a river. He followed along the bank. The area was strangely calm and quiet, apart from the constant buzzing around his ears from the mosquitoes. He marvelled at the landscape and ever-changing weather. He could be soaked by rain or fried by the sun. he was nothing in his immense jungle. In his entire life, he never felt so insignificant. The silence was later broken when he came across two fishermen landing their small-motorized canoe.

They eyed him suspiciously as they tied the small craft to a tree. "Con lai," the older one shouted and waved his hand angrily at Jason. He picked up a small rock and hurled in Jason's direction.

"Oi, watch it! That nearly hit me," Jason

shouted back. The taller, younger fisherman picked up a stick and ran towards Jason.

"Con lai! Con lai!" he shouted again. He attempted to strike Jason with the stick; Jason ducked and swept his attackers feet away from him, sending him down to the ground. The stunned fisherman sat on the ground, his pride hurt more than anything when his older friend started laughing.

"Stay down, Captain Ahab, if you don't want to get hurt" Jason said. "And while we are at it, stop calling me half-breed. That's racist."

The fisherman climbed to his feet. e took out his fishing knife and approached, trying to scare the boy away.

"Seriously, you're gonna try and stab me now?" Jason asked with his hands on his hips. He studied the knife. It was thin towards the tip, suggesting it had been sharpened many times. He ran at the man and leapt into the air. He threw a kick and caught the man in the face. He grabbed the man's wrist as he fell and twisted, causing the man to scream in pain and drop the knife.

The older fisherman approached cautiously with a fishing pole pointing at Jason.

"And all this because you think I'm a half-breed?" Jason cursed in disbelief although neither man could understand him. Rather than carry on fighting Jason took the easy option He pulled out the pistol that was tucked inside his belt and aimed it at both men. Immediately, they held their hands above their heads.

"Go run," Jason shouted he gestured with the pistol. Both men understood and ran off into the dense undergrowth. They had no idea what the boy was saying but were smart enough to run when they had the chance.

He was pleased with himself when he worked out how to start the little motor on the canoe. He picked up his backpack and cast off. The canoe didn't go very fast, but it was much easier than walking, and he was sure he would be able to get to Tay Ninh before the fast approaching deadline. Jason still had no plan on how to find the actual prison or how to free his father but was sure he would think of something when he needed to.

Chapter Eighteen

The following morning, a five-man team from the Vietnamese army searched the river for the gun-toting boy. They never found him. The Vietnamese army was told to keep a watch out for him. Jason had travelled over forty miles before the early hours of the morning.

Dark rain clouds had blocked the moonlight and made it absolute darkness. It seemed to fold in on all sides around him and made it dangerous to keep going. He found a suitable place under a fallen tree to hide and tie up to. He slept in the canoe, spending much of the night swatting mosquitoes that fancied his blood.

Jason ate some of the fruit he had bought from the market the day before and drank a bottle of his water. He knew he would eventually have to drink the river water with the purification tablets but wanted to put it off for as long as possible. Earlier he had noticed a dead cow in the water that was rotten and full of maggots. He didn't relish the thought of drinking from the same source.

After studying his map, he worked out he was back in Cambodia. So far he had only seen a few fishing canoes. Often he waved, getting nothing back in return other than a nod, and that's the way he preferred it as he continued up stream. Unknown to him, three patrol boats were heading down river in his direction. One of them was carrying General Chow. He was really disappointed when the war ended with the United States. He enjoyed the action, killing Americans and torturing them. Part of him still believed that the war was raging on.

*

Back in the United States, Max gathered the reports from Thailand. News of the stolen aircraft being flown by a blond haired boy had also broken in the UK and US. The information that it was forced down and had to make a crash landing on a beach in Vietnam concerned Max. The Vietnamese official statement was they were still looking for the pilot. Max was unsure if that was true and wondered if Jason had got away or had himself been taken prisoner.

Max contacted SYUI in London and spoke to George Young again. George had called Scott Turner but he had not heard from Jason either. Scott played sick and was allowed to stay home from school. He wanted to monitor his ham radio. A year earlier Jason contacted him while in Jakarta via Morse code. Scott hoped if Jason was alive he may try the same thing.

*

The river meandered back into Vietnam. Jason was getting low on fuel and knew it was only a matter of time before he would be forced to ditch the canoe and continue on foot. He rounded a bend and his engine started to splutter, eventually stopping. He tried in vain, pulling on the starter rope, to start it, but without fuel it refused. Pausing and catching his breath, he thought he could hear something. He listened hard and heard it again. It was a motorboat. *Good they can tow me to shore,* he said to himself.

As the boat approached, Jason was horrified to discover it was a Vietnamese Army armoured motor launch with at least five soldiers on board. He ensured his gun was well hidden under his shirt and waved at them. They ignored his pleasant smile and pulled alongside. One kept his automatic rifle pointing at Jason.

They shouted something at him. He pointed at his mouth and acted dumb. Again they shouted. Jason smiled and held out his hand. He pointed at his mouth and shook his head. They seem to understand that he could not speak, but one still climbed on to his canoe and searched it. He came across Jason's backpack. Jason dreaded what they might find. The solider shouted and he pulled out the map, compass, and three grenades. Another two guns pointed at Jason from the crew of the motorboat.

The solider held the grenades under Jason's face and shouted at him. He pointed in the undergrowth, pretending he had found them. The guard struck Jason across his face, knocking the boy down on his back. Jason pointed again at the undergrowth. Eventually, they seemed to understand that he had found them. As they were used and American, they assumed he had come across them in the jungle. It was not uncommon for locals and children to find weapons and other military items, even dead bodies, left behind from the war. Very often children would step on a land mine and get killed or seriously injured.

The solider took his backpack; Jason stood and protested. He knew he needed the map. He jumped across onto the launch and held out his hand for the items. They laughed at him and pushed him back. One of the soldiers on the boat who Jason suspected was in charge said something to another and pointed at Jason. He wanted him searched. They suspected he was Amerasian, after all, they had come across thousands of them. But this boy was very fair and had sapphire blue eyes and not a hint of Asian.

He bent down and started to search Jason. It would only be a matter of moments when they discovered the gun he had on him.

Jason caught the soldier's collar with his left hand and pulled the soldier towards him. At the same time Jason unleashed a blow with his right fist. He hit his target, the man's windpipe. It happened too quickly for the others to react. He leapt forward grabbed a grenade and pulled out the pin and held it shut. They all froze, afraid to move. Just their eyes followed him. The officer in charge tried to calm Jason down. He smiled. The others kept their guns aimed at the boy. They knew if they shot him he would drop the grenade with the pin out and they would all die.

Jason has never used a grenade before. He wondered how long it took to go off once he let it go and released the trigger mechanism. *What if it goes off instantly*? He tried to act calm, but deep down he was more terrified of the grenade than they were.

He gestured for them to lower the weapons. Slowly they lowered them. He beckoned them to step onto the canoe. One by one they clambered aboard the small-motorized canoe. The officer tried to stay, but Jason picked up a second grenade and gestured again. It was enough to move him off the launch. When they were all on his canoe he untied it and pushed it off, this was the most frightening part. He knew as soon as they far enough away not to get hurt by the grenade they would open fire.

After looking over the boat's control panel, Jason threw it towards the forward arrow. The launch slowly started moving. He placed the other lever at full power. The engine roared, and the propeller churned the brown murky water behind the boat. Jason threw one grenade into the canoe and the second grenade into the water behind him. He ducked down and covered his head with his arms.

Chaos erupted in the canoe as the soldiers tripped over each other trying to pick up the grenade, the second grenade exploded in the water, throwing up water all over the men. Eventually they found the grenade that Jason tossed into the canoe.

It still had the pin in it and was harmless, but it did as he intended and caused enough distraction to get clear. The water soaked men screamed abuse at Jason. Two of them opened fire.

A few bullets hit the motor launch, but the Vietnamese soldiers all standing on the canoe caused it to wobble. They were unable to get a good shot. Jason stayed down and waited for the pounding of bullets to subside. They continued and increased coming from another direction. He poked his head up to take a look. They were no longer shooting at him from behind. He crouched down and was relieved his grenade hurt no one. He crawled to the front of the launch so he could peek a view over the front. To his horror, he was heading directly for another Vietnamese launch.

The main machine gunner was pounding Jason's launch with bullets. Two other soldiers also fired their automatic weapons at him. He had just moments before they collided. He placed the last grenade next to two five-gallon Jerrycans full of gas. The other launch was getting perilously close to Jason's. He could hear them shouting. They assumed he was shot. He pulled the pin of the grenade and, at the last second, steered it into the path of the other launch. Seconds before it collided, he jumped up and dived deep into the water.

It felt warm and sluggish, covered with a layer of rotten vegetation. It was like jumping into the dirty bath water of whole football team. The water was scummy and dark green and smelt awful. As Jason broke the water's surface, he could feel the green slime and algae running down his cheek and over his lips.

He took a breath and swam deep a powerful breaststroke that took him deeper. Something whizzed past near him, and he realized that he was still being shot at. The farther down he went, the safer he would be. As he pushed himself down, he wondered what creatures might be in the water. Crocodiles? Piranha fish? Pythons? He could barely see two or three inches into the water's murky depths. His thoughts were quickly dispelled when the two motor launches collided with a crash. A few seconds later a huge explosion erupted. It was deafening to him under the water. With his body crying out for oxygen, Jason pushed himself up towards the surface. He expelled his air and desperately kicked upwards. He gasped at the air once he broke the surface.

Heat from the burning wreckages stung his face; his heart sank as he noticed some bodies floating lifeless on the water. Some men were alive and helping the wounded. He turned, put his head down, and swam for the opposite shore. The swim was exhausting. His clothing weighed him down, and he had lost his hat. He finally got to shallow water and started to stride out towards the shore and among the reeds.

A third launch rounded the corner. Standing on the front with folded arms was General Chow. The launch immediately opened fire with machine guns. The water around Jason came alive as bullets pounded the surface. It was only a matter of time before he was hit. He dove back under the water after taking a deep breath. The water above was still pounded with bullets as he swam back out to deeper water. He poked his head up for a second to get a breath and noticed the man with a patch over his eye. General Chow looked right at him and pointed.

Jason thought he looked like a pirate as the bullets hit the surface again. Jason dove down to the riverbed and scuttled along the bottom. The boat drew closer, slicing through the water.

Jason pulled a large reed out of the riverbed, cut the end off with his knife, and blew down it. Before he could congratulate himself on his brilliant idea, another burst of gunfire spat across the water in his direction. He dove back down into the water and used it as a snorkel to breathe.

General Chow's launch got closer as it searched in vain for the boy. It came almost on top of him. Chow raised his hand and the shooting ceased. He looked around the area with his hands stuck on his hips, looking presidential.

He continued to search for the boy; he wanted to see his dead body. He remained on the front of the boat shooting at anything that made a ripple in the water. A frog, a fish, he didn't care. Someone had to pay for killing and injuring his men.

After an hour they gave up. They assumed he had been shot or drowned. General Chow cursed and spat. For good measure, he threw some grenades into the water. They waited, but a few dead fish and a turtle floated to the surface; no boy. Jason had travelled further downstream and was out of harm's way.

Jason waited until he heard the motor launch's engine disappear before his head broke the surface of the water to take a look. He was safe for now, although he had used up much of his energy. He was relieved to eventually get back on shore. He still had his map, his gun, and compass but had lost his backpack.

He tore the sleeve off his shirt and tied it around his head like a bandana. He hoped it would cover his blond hair and make him look less like a westerner. At least it had stopped raining, he thought as he looked up. The sun was riding high across a blue sky decorated with puffy clouds. All the scents of Vietnam drifted in—the smell of the trees and rotting vegetation in the jungle, the sharp tang of the river.

He sat and rested in deep thought, reflecting on the day. The dead bodies caused by his actions lay heavily on his mind. When he had last talked with his mentor Wong Tong he asked how he could forget the death he caused because it was still happening every time he closed his eyes and tried to sleep. Wong Tong had told him, "There are two kinds of people Jason. Those who save lives, and those who take lives. You, young Jason, fall into a different category, one who save lives by taking lives."

It gave Jason some comfort.

Chapter Nineteen

The nine remaining prisoners were marched out of the cell. They were forced to kneel in a line. A Vietnamese guard prodded them with his rifle. He hit the American journalist harder because the scene was being filmed. The film would later be shown on TV news stations around the world. Many commentators asked why the US, British, and French governments has not intervened.

Ray Steed stared straight ahead. He was unsure if Jason would be watching. He wanted to ensure that the last time his son watched him he would not be showing any fear. A few others sobbed. Some simply held their heads down. As far as Ray was concerned, Jason was safely tucked away at the American military academy.

*

The BBC showed the news in the UK the following day. Scott Turner watched with his parents. He fought back his tears as he watched his best friend's father appear unafraid and defiant in the face of death. He had heard from George that Jason was missing and hoped that his friend would soon make contact.

News stations showed the news across the United States. Members of Congress met with the president. All agreed nothing could be done. All US personnel were ordered to leave the area. Even the Red Cross pulled out of Vietnam in fear of the volunteers being captured and facing the same fate.

The prisoners were marched back to the cell. All of them looked defeated. They chatted, trying to lift each other's spirits. They spoke of family, what countries they had visited, and wondered when the Americans would rescue them.

French Captain Marcel Deschamps argued that the Americans would not be coming. He told them that if France's great Foreign Legion couldn't defeat the Vietnamese then no one would be able too. It was no wonder the Americans left with their tails between their legs. The British prisoners, including Ray, doubted that Great Britain would send in the SAS. It was getting more likely that they would either be released after negotiations or they would remain prisoners or be executed.

Captain Marcel and many of the other prisoners respected Raymond Steed. They admired how he kept calm, never complained, and always tried to look on the positive side to keep everyone from falling into complete despair. Marcel was a large, proud Frenchman. Io look at him it was hard to guess his age. He kept his hair completely shaven, and his moustache was grey. It made him look a lot older than his thirty-one years.

"So tell me, Lieutenant Steed. Do you have a

pretty wife and family waiting for you in England?" Marcel asked.

Ray smiled and looked up at Marcel. "No. My wife passed away giving birth to our son. He is twelve now." Ray's eyes welled up as he thought of his son being made an orphan.

Marcel picked up on it, for once Ray was as human as the rest of them. "Who looks after your son when you are away with the Royal Navy?"

"We have a housekeeper, and Jason sort of takes care of himself now. He's actually in a military academy in America. He's a cadet and, from what I heard before this, he was doing just great."

"In the US you say? What academy does he go to?" Carl Bradley, the American journalist, asked.

"It's called Quentin Roosevelt Military Academy. Somewhere in Dakota." Ray smiled.

"Wow, QRMA. That's in South Dakota. It's the country's top academy. Only the very best go there. You have to be top of another academy in your year just to be able to apply. A few presidents went there and probably some future presidents as well. How did he get in? No offence but he's a Brit and you don't have any military academies."

Ray grinned and felt proud of his son. "He's not your average twelve-year-old boy. He was in Jakarta as a Sea Cadet eighteen months ago when the massacre happened. He was one of the lucky ones. He ended up on Jakarta—" Ray stopped short.

To explain all of Jason's adventures sounded so farfetched it would be hard to believe. "He was chosen because of that and a few other things."

"Oh I get it. To show you British how we do things," Carl Bradley said. "Good for the Quentin Roosevelt Military Academy to allow a Brit in. Still, he must find it hard. The competition among the other cadets is such a high standard. How does he keep up?"

"I think Jason can keep up with the others just fine." Ray rested his head back against the brick wall and closed his eyes. He could picture Jason throwing his school backpack across the highly polished floor and kicking his shoes off and leaving them wherever they landed. Ray himself was given a strict up bringing; the huge house they lived in was always quiet, spotlessly clean, and rather boring.

Ray tried to be strict but now Jason was living at the house. Lights were left on in every room he went into, the TV was left on, and if he was in his room, you could hear his music from down stairs. The housekeeper cleaned his room, but Jason would leave his clothing spread across the floor and dirty food dishes everywhere. The fridge had to be stocked with his favourite food, carrot cake. Ray thought to himself he would swap his right arm if he could watch Jason throw his school backpack and kick his shoes off across the floor again.

*

Jason's long trek through the jungle was taking its toll on him. He was certain he was being followed and kept up a pace that Corporal Armstrong would have been proud of.

Suddenly, a high pitch whizz sounded past his ear, a crackle of machine-gun fire. Jason ducked and thought he heard someone shout, but when he looked around, there was no one there. That was the most unnerving thing, to be shot at in the middle of the jungle with not a single one of the Vietcong actually visible. A tree had caught fire. The entire trunk was wrapped in flames and thick smoke. They had fired a mortar at him.

Jason caught sight of a barbed wire fence. He headed towards it, knowing it was man-made meant there could be shelter a place to hide. Jason broke into a sprint. He reached the fence. It carried another sign written in English, French and what he assumed was Vietnamese. DANGER, KEEP OUT. Jason almost smiled. What danger could possibly be worse than being shot at by machine guns and a mortar? As if to answer the question, there were two more explosions no more than thirty feet behind him.

He leapt over the fence and continued running for his life. He slowed and looked behind him. He continued on. He was getting close to a steep riverbank. He could just see the water. His foot came down on something metallic. He heard-and felt-it click underneath his boot, He stopped in disbelief and looked down. His entire body was screaming at him to run away. He had learnt about land mines at QRMA. He remembered some had a two second delay mechanism, but was also told that some of the pressure sensitive switches had no delay and would go off as soon as your foot was lifted.

Jason stood there. At least he was not being followed and shot at. He could imagine the sudden flash, the terrific pain, his foot being separated from his body. And worst, there was nothing he could do. His foot was glued to a deadly device. If he died here, his father would never know how far he had gotten. He thought back to his training. "Always look beyond what you can see." Wong Tong always told him.

Jason took in his surroundings. The mine had been placed on the top of a ridge, the ground sloping away steeply to the river at the bottom. Jason tried to work out the distances. If he threw himself sideways. Could he reach the bottom before the mine exploded? And if the force of the blast was above him, would he escape the worst of it? Jason momentarily smiled. *Maybe I should have paid more attention to that algebra stuff.*

The shooting had stopped. Everything was very still and quiet. He built up an adrenaline rush into his body. His pupils dilated, his body flushed with blood and perspired, each muscle fiber contracting like a coiled spring. Jason had to force himself, knowing that he might be making the worst mistake of his life, that in seconds from now he could be crippled, and would die an agonizing death.

He jumped.

At the very last moment, he had doubts, but

it was too late. He continued anyway, launching himself into the air and down the slope with all his strength. He thought he felt the mine vibrate very slightly as his foot left it. But it hadn't exploded, at least not in the first second that he left the mine. The slope was rushing past him, a dark streak at the corner of his eye. Then he hit the river. Water, warm and inviting, submerged his body. Behind him an explosion. The mine. Clumps of earth and vegetation rained down on him. Then nothing. He was underwater. The fuse must have given him two seconds and those two seconds saved him.

Jason swam forward when there was another movement just outside the field of his vision. He strained his eyes to see its image. Puzzled, he looked up. And froze. He actually felt the air stop somewhere deep in his lungs. The last of the bubbles chased each other to the surface. Jason hung there, fighting for control. He wanted to scream, but underwater that was impossible.

He was looking up at a Siamese Crocodile at least thirteen feet long, circling above him. The sight was so unreal, so terrifying, that at first Jason quite literally didn't believe his eyes. It had to be an illusion, some sort of trick. The very fact that it was so close to him seemed impossible. He stared at the cream coloured underbelly, the large clawed feet, the teeth projecting from its prehistoric mouth. And there were the deadly, round eyes, as black and as primitive as anything on the planet. Had they seen him yet?

Jason forced himself not to breathe. His

heart was pounding. Not just his heart, his whole body. He once faced a leopard. That was scary but, this... The simple truth was that he was terrified. He had never been so scared in his life.

What did he know about crocodiles? What could he do? Slowly, he pulled out his gun. Would it work in water? Or would the water slow the bullet down so much it couldn't penetrate the thick leather skin of the crocodile? Suddenly, it moved. It was coming. It's monstrous tail thrashed, foaming water behind it as it came closer.

"Gaa." Jason blew in desperation. He pushed up towards the oncoming crocodile and aimed. The gun worked, much to his thanks. Three shots into the crocodile. The water came alive as Jason forced himself up past it, desperate to catch the one thing he needed more than anything. Air.

The crocodile twitched, bubbles and foaming blood stained the churning waters crimson. Jason's head broke the surface of the water he sucked in as much air as he could, filling his hungry lungs. He swam for the shoreline. A few strokes and he was there. He climbed out and ran, not looking back, unsure if the Vietcong had heard the gunshots. How could they not have? They were the loudest thing he had ever heard. He was almost deafened by the gun. Jason never stopped running for another hour until his body begged him for food.

It was a hard march through the jungle and swamp. The days were always hot. He concentrated on the heat and fatigue and the simple motions of the hike. It went that way for hours. One leg, the next leg, his legs counted the hours. Jason thought it was a dirty, tangled country. Empty villages. No people, no dogs, or chickens. Deep hedges and bush flanked the trail with slow curves hiding possible dangers.

He heard voices, or was it birds chatting and laughing at him? Was he losing his mind? He had been shot at, almost blown apart, and attacked by a crocodile. "What's next?" Jason asked himself. "Okay, so now you're talking to yourself. That's the first sign of madness."

At night a new fear set in. The moonlight cascaded great shadows through the tress of spooks and goblins. They watched him sleep, occasionally slapping a mosquito on his face.

Daybreak, same smells, more rain. It was the heat that woke him. Then the flies. Jason wondered what the day would bring. His feet hurt as he trampled through a never-ending sea of lush vegetation. "Maybe I will die today. Flies will lay eggs up my nose and maggots will crawl out of my ears just like the dead cow in the river. I will rot and become part of the mud in this rotten, stinking over-heated jungle," he whispered to himself.

Rain dripped from his blond hair. Falling onto his face past his eyes, down his neck, and splattering onto his shirt, then running down his body and even soaking his boxer shorts. They clung to his skin, heavy and clammy beneath his trousers. He knew there would be leeches clinging to his legs, arms, back, and chest beneath his clothes, even though he couldn't feel them. They were small and thin before they started sucking his blood. He would discover them later as he tried to wash, swollen with his blood.

Jason longed to strip off and take a warm shower and dry off in a fluffy warm towel. His thoughts wondered from fresh talcum powder to carrot cake and more food. Food. He needed it. Using his mental notes he started to search for something.

"No way am I eating *you*," Jason said screwing up his face at the Sago Grub he fished out the bark of a palm tree. The two inch thick creamy white grub was as large as his thumb. He had been taught at the academy that the Sago Grub was the larva of the Palm Weevil. It was full of nutrients that he needed. It wriggled between his thumb and forefinger; he gently placed it back in a crevice of the bark.

He was hungry and knew he had to eat something. So far, all he managed to find was two unripe mangos. His body was getting tired and it needed protein. It had recently rained so he had been able to collect rainwater in a make shift funnel of leaves. Despite his hunger, the thought of eating grubs repulsed him.

It was getting tougher to concentrate on freeing his father. He was very alone, miles from anyone, deep in the Vietnamese Jungle with no radio ad no food. Even his watch had packed up on him.

Using the map and compass, he was sure he was just a few miles from Tay Ninh, and if his information was correct, this was where the prisoners were being held.

The rain had stopped as suddenly as it had started. Jason could hear the water still gurgling down the trees and a few last drops pattering on the leaves. He was soaked again.

Jason stopped. He heard a strange sound. It was a welcoming sound. For two days all he had heard was the rain or the constant chatter of birds and crickets. This sounded like children singing. He crept through the undergrowth towards the sound. Peering through the lush green canopy, he could see a small village. Maybe twelve homes and some fencing with a few chickens in a pen, another area housed some dogs. A goat was tied to a tree stump on the outskirts eating grass.

In the center was a larger building, built mostly from bamboo with a group of thirty or so children sitting in a group cross-legged and singing. Jason assumed it was a school. He crept closer to get a better look. He was unsure if it was safe to approach. He doubted they had a telephone, so news of the incident with patrol launches would not have reached here. However, just to be safe, he thought he would wait and observe.

Chapter Twenty

In Scotland, Jason's grandparents were given news that Jason had gone missing from the academy. With Jason's father being held captive, his grandparents were his next of kin. His grandparents, although concerned, were not too anxious. They had fretted over Jason disappearing before and, although they thought he was too young to be off helping SYUI, he always seems to scrape through. They had now come to realize that he was no ordinary boy with ordinary problems such as school or behavioural. Jason always had bigger issues, such as being shot at, or being chased across Europe by Triads and then there was the time he had to jump from a moving cable car or swim from shark infested waters. Ever since he was five and he dived into the fishpond of Buckingham Palace to rescue the four-year-old princess he had always seemed to find trouble.

*

Jason shook his watch, trying to get it to start. He was hungry, tired, and for once, unsure what to do. He needed food. He hoped that once the school finished he could break in and find some food and water and move on to find his father. He never really had the time to wait but was too weak to carry on. The high humidity and temperature sapped his strength. He slept on and off for a few hours.

Eventually, the children left the classrooms but stayed close to the school. They gathered in small groups and played a game Jason had never seen before. They stood in a line behind each other and held the person in front's belt or back of his or her pants. They made what looked like a long snake of children. One stood at the front talking, then suddenly he ran, trying to grab the tail of the snake or in this case, the last boy. The children ran, following the leader and trying to block the boy who wanted the tail.

They screamed with laughter as he got closer only to be blocked by the twisting snake's body. Jason smiled as he watched them enjoying themselves with their strange game. A few children sat out and chatted; two older boys kicked a stone back and forth like soccer. Jason couldn't wait anymore; he slowly strolled over to the play area.

Two girls noticed him and smiled. Jason thought they were about eight, maybe older but they were very thin. Their clothing was almost rag torn grey shorts and washed out blue shirts. He smiled at them, causing them to giggle and run away. An older boy around Jason's age approached. Jason smiled giving a big show of his brilliant white teeth and nodded at the boy. He soon realized that they were all Amerasian children. The boy approaching had slightly oriental eyes but had light brown hair and western features.

He said something to Jason in Vietnamese. Jason tried speaking English and Chinese, but neither worked. He settled for sign language and motioned his mouth and his stomach, signalling he was hungry. The boy smiled and nodded. He took Jason's hand and led him inside. Jason took in his surroundings. The large room had blankets laid out on the floor, each blanket with a rolled up cloth for pillow. He was unsure why the school would have beds for all the children. He was introduced to an older woman. She seemed to be in charge.

The woman was thin. Jason thought she looked about sixty. She wore a cross on a chain around her neck and a plain black dress. He assumed she was a nun or something like one. She spoke in Vietnamese. The boy spoke to her and informed her Jason could not speak Vietnamese.

Jason tried Chinese and English. To his surprise she spoke back in French and called herself Claudette

"You're French?" Jason asked in French.

"Yes, I am. Can you speak French as well?" She asked. Jason was pleased he could finally communicate with someone. She wrongly assumed he had been thrown out of his home or village like all the other children. This was an orphanage for Amerasian children; the few orphanages in Vietnam would not always allow Amerasian children to stay. If it was not for a few places like this, many

Amerasian children would be left to fend for themselves. She believed she was doing God's work and was the children's, teacher, guardian, cook, and nurse.

He was given a stew of vegetables and meat. The meat was scarce; he only came across one small piece. He felt better after eating and drinking until he asked what the meat was. It was the first and, he hoped, last time he would ever eat dog again. He was annoyed with himself for eating it. He had seen it earlier but was so tired and hungry he just forgot. She offered to make Jason up a bed for the night, but he told her he couldn't stay he needed to find the prison camp.

Claudette refused to give him the whereabouts at first eventually, she gave in and told him that a few locals had mentioned an older prison camp by the Suoi Da River. He pulled out his map; she started to show him on the map, until she noticed it was stamped *Property of the US Army*. After flashing his winning adorable smile and some persuasion, she showed him where the locals had mentioned where the prison was. He was given food and water for his journey and said goodbye to Claudette. Even after he left she was unsure if he was telling her the truth. His story seemed a little far-fetched.

A blood-curdling scream, followed by more screams and shouts, came from the lower end of the village. The caged dogs barked, the roar of a truck engine broke the sleepy quiet village. Two troop-carrying trucks followed by a small armoured personal carrier stopped in the village center. General Chow stepped out and dusted himself off; he stood with his hands on his hips and watched as his troops disembarked.

An officer barked orders, the troops started searching each home. The terrified villagers were being rounded up.

"Jason, you had better leave," Claudette warned. "Go out the back. God will protect you."

Jason nodded and ran into the dense undergrowth. He wanted to hide and see what happened. Maybe he could help. But knew he was seriously outnumbered and was totally unaware of why General Chow had come to the village. He thought it best to take Claudette's advice and leave while he still could.

General Chow forced the villagers to stand in three rows while he inspected them. When he came to the children he spat on the floor in disgust. He pushed a small boy out of his way so he could barge past. The boy, no more than four-years-old, fell to the ground.

Claudette objected. Within seconds she had six rifles pointed at her. "They are just children," she pleaded.

"Children of the dust, children of the enemy," General Chow shouted at her.

"They are also half Vietnamese, but more importantly they are just children, God's children," she argued. The boy ran to her and hugged her legs.

"We are looking for one particular Amerasian boy. We tracked him here. He has blue eyes and blond hair. Tell us where we can find him, and you can live in piece with these disgusting vermin children," General Chow said. His one eye glared at Claudette.

"These *are* all the children. The last one to join us was Huong. She has been with us for a month now." Claudette stroked the head of an eight-year-old girl. "As God as my witness, I have seen no boy as you describe, General."

General Chow paced up and down, staring at the children and villagers. His troops had finished the search of the village and had found nothing.

"When I catch this boy, he will be tortured and questioned. If he *has* been here, we will be back and will squash this village." General Chow snarled, waving his fist as if he was squashing a bug in his hand. He gave the orders, and the troops climbed back on the trucks. Within minutes they were gone, trying to track the Amerasian blond haired boy.

Jason had only travelled two hundred meters. He was aware he was being followed. He ducked down into the undergrowth and waited, listening to his follower's feet scuffle on the ground of fallen leaves. It was two of the children he had seen them at the orphanage, a boy and girl about nine. They looked similar, and Jason thought they might be twins. After they passed and he was sure they were alone, he followed them. They turned and smiled when they saw him.

"What do you want? Why are you following me?" Jason asked. They said nothing and took his hand. Reluctantly, he went with them. They took him deeper into the jungle and stopped by a large fallen tree trunk. They moved some palm leaves that had been carefully placed to conceal a bamboo covered hole and climbed down into the ground.

Jason followed them down an underground tunnel; it was damp, muddy, and full of crawling bugs. They turned on an oil lamp and went farther down into the tunnel on hands and knees. He followed them farther along, every few paces they had to clamber over tree roots that had grown into the tunnel.

They came to an opening; Jason was amazed at how large it was. It opened up to a large room with two more passageways going off in other directions. The girl lifted a secret door in the ground and climbed down. The boy gestured Jason to follow. He felt uneasy, but he trusted the two children and followed her into the lower level. Her brother passed down the oil lamp. When the light came down, Jason gasped. The secret room was full of weapons. He examined them and found them to be mostly American.

They had been collected by the Vietnamese army and hidden. After the war, they had been forgotten. Jason picked up a semi-automatic Smith & Wesson Model 39. He looked it over. It wasn't too large for his hands. When he checked the clip he saw it was fully loaded. Jason made himself busy. He filled six more clips with 9mm bullets. Once he had finished, he picked up a holster and belt. He had to use his knife to cut a new hole so it would fit him, since it was made for an adult.

His eyes darted around the room, looking for something else. He picked up a belt full of hand grenades. It was too heavy for his slim waist so he put it over his head then scooped up an M18 Claymore mine. It came complete with a long wire and blasting cap. Jason thought it seemed simple to use. On the front it had the words 'Front toward Enemy.' He took two of those and packed them in his backpack. Finally, he picked up a grenade launcher. It was heavy and had no instructions on how to use it. After a few seconds stroking it, he placed it back It was too heavy and cumbersome to take into the jungle.

"This is all I need, thanks," Jason said to the twins. They both smiled at him and laughed as they watched him struggle to squeeze back up to the room above with the grenades around his neck. "Don't bloody laugh. If these go off in here, they'll hear the bang back in London."

They smiled at him, not sure what he had just said to them.

Once they got outside, Jason thanked them both. He felt sorry for them. Stuck at the orphanage with little chance of being adopted and hated the local people because of their western appearance. It made Jason think about the runaway children at the

Chicken Ranch. They had no idea how lucky they were to be British rather than born in Vietnam, fathered by an American who was either dead or gone home to his American life.

Chapter Twenty-One

The United States held an emergency meeting at the Pentagon. It included the US President Gerald Ford and Vice President Rockefeller along with the head of the CIA. The defence minister from Great Britain had arrived, along with his French counterpart. Gough Whitlam, the Australian Prime Minister, had also flown to the United States to attend the meeting. They sat along a forty-foot table; the Chief of Staff sat to the right of the US President. The twenty-seven men were introduced to Max Fisher.

Max marched up to a large screen. He was smartly dressed in an Italian suit. He held a large wooden ruler. The screen turned on and showed a picture of the ten captured prisoners that was taken a few days before when all ten were still alive.

"We still have some sources in South Vietnam. Our information is sketchy to say the least, but it's all we have.' He paused and took a breath, almost afraid to say what he was about to announce. "It is possible we have a plan B," Max said.

"I won't put another US soldier's foot in

Vietnam," President Ford insisted.

"No sir, you don't have to. It's a British foot." Max smiled.

"What? It's a bit late to plan anything now. We have less than twenty-four hours." British Defence Secretary, Roy Mason, choked. His huge eyebrows rose higher than his hairline.

"We think he's already there, Sir," Max said the interruptions were annoying him. "Three days ago Jason Steed disappeared from Quentin Roosevelt Military Academy." Max clicked a hand held switch and a picture of Jason wearing his Sea Cadet uniform appeared on the screen. A rumble went around the room.

"Is this a bloody joke mate? He's a kid!" argued the Australian Prime Minister. The room fell silent when Roy got up from his chair and walked closer to the screen. He jabbed his finger back and forth towards Jason's image and nodded before sitting back down again.

"I know of him and what he is capable of. Carry on, Fisher," Roy said.

Max cleared his throat. "We believe he stowed away on an aircraft that flew from the military airfield across the street from the academy. Jason Steed was given a pass so he could workout with some of the security staff."

President Ford interrupted him. "What kind of idiot gave him a security pass?" he snarled, looking at Max, who turned red, cleared his throat, and, ignoring the Presidents question, carried on.

"Jason Steed is an expert in martial arts. Well, to cut a long story short a boy fitting his description assaulted a guard at U-Tapao Pattaya International Airport in Thailand. He was asking questions about the prisoners. A few minutes later a small plane was stolen and—" He was interrupted again.

"You're not suggesting this boy, Steed, stole an aircraft?" scoffed President Ford.

"Yes, Sir. He holds a pilot's license." He paused. "Let me take you back eighteen months ago. Jakarta. The Sea Cadet that recovered the missile arming cassette, freed the prisoners, and flew them out on a vintage bomber and landed it in Australia?" Max said.

"Is this the same boy?" President Ford asked, getting up from his seat and looking closer at the image on the screen.

"Yes, Sir. Since then, he has been working with SYUI and MI6, undercover of course. He was also the inside person that gave SYUI information on the Coco Bites Scandal by the Triads. However, this time, of course, he's working alone as it's personal. The plane he stole from U-Tapao Pattaya International Airport was forced down on a beach in South Vietnam. The pilot was never found and then another incident happened. Two days ago two Vietnamese army armoured boats were destroyed. From what information we can gather, a blond haired, blue-eyed boy aged around twelve forced the crew off one with a grenade and used it to ram another while leaving a live grenade. One man died and one is seriously injured. We believe that boy to be the very same Jason Steed, and like I said, this time it's personal."

"Exactly why is it personal?" Roy asked. "Isn't this just Jason Steed doing what he does best?"

"No, sir. He's working alone. It's not a planned mission. It's personal because one of the British prisoners, Lieutenant Raymond Steed, is Jason's father."

The room fell silent again for a few moments. Eventually, Roy stood. "The British government does not use children on missions, Fisher. He was on vacation in Jakarta with another one hundred Sea cadets when that went off. We were all lucky that the boy was there and got caught up in it."

"And the Triad Coco Bites Mission or the more recent mission where he helped close down a child abduction gang? Did he just get caught up in that as well?" Max scoffed.

"Hmmm, good point. Well, however it seems, this time he's on his own. What are his chances?" Roy asked.

"We have no more information. At this point, we don't know if he is even still alive. If he is, he will be making his way towards Tay Ninh. Our information leads us to believe this is where the prison camp is."

"How would this twelve-year-old boy, staying at one of our academies, get hold of that information?" Vice President Rockefeller asked.

Max turned and stared at Roy. "Because he asked the head of SYUI, a Mr. George Young. Apparently Mr. Young didn't think it would do any harm and has a soft spot for the boy."

Roy squirmed in his chair. He faked a cough before stiffing up again.

"So that's your plan B? You have a twelve-year-old old boy working alone trying to help his dad, but for now we have no idea if he is alive, dead, or just out surfing," the Australian Prime Minster said. "What you're saying is he's the only chance we have of us getting the men out? What are his chances one or two percent? If you ask me, not much of a plan B."

"This is the same boy who rescued the marines off Jakarta and crash landed the aircraft at Broomfield Airfield and managed to get the cassette back to stop the nuclear warhead going off. He is the youngest person in Britain to hold a pilot's license. He has been awarded the VC and is a black belt in various karate disciplines. He's smart, fit, and determined. He has probably more chance than any adult agent we could send because no one would suspect him," Fisher argued.

"Agreed, but he will leave a trail of bodies behind him. After the Coca Bites affair, the Triads swore revenge on him. Many members of the public got caught up in the crossfire. Don't expect him to ask for his father's release nicely. He will take down anyone who gets in his way." Roy said.

"Well gentlemen, for everyone's sake, let's hope he's still alive and can help the prisoners. His mission is personal and has nothing to do with the United States. If the media heard about this they would have a field day. As it is, they're calling our troops 'Baby Killers.' I will pray for him," President Ford said.

"He's British, Sir it won't come back on us," Fisher suggested.

"Yes it will. He's a student at an American military academy. You know how the media would put a spin on it. Whatever the outcome, we must keep this under wraps."

Chapter Twenty-Two

Jason found the journey hard work. The jungle was dense. He had to climb through palm trees, bamboo, and thick, luscious foliage. To make matters worse, a thunderstorm erupted in the sky. He was soaked to the skin. It rained so hard the ground eventually became mud. He squelched and splashed forward, pausing every now and then to examine his compass. His feet started to suffer as they rubbed against the wet leather of his boots.

The arduous journey never stopped his determination to keep going forward. Lightning lit up the sky. The crushing rain was so deafening he never heard the thunder that followed. Jason couldn't hear anything but the crushing rain. He had a comforting thought that if he couldn't hear anything then neither could anyone else.

He came across a small river. While looking for an easier place to cross, he noticed a large flat bottom barge tied up to the bank. He climbed on board. It was empty but sound. He guessed it was used to transport troops up and down the river during the war. As he examined it, he noticed it had no engine but was floating and quite stable. *Would have been perfect if it had an engine* he said to himself as he jumped off and waded across the river.

*

The nine remaining prisoners huddled together, trying to avoid the worst of the leaks in the roof. They were only given water this morning. Today, they had not even been fed the rotten mangos or maggot infested bread that they normally were given. Ray had watched the others break down one by one. Some would actually cry, some would rant and rave, others just sat quietly and prayed with tears in their eyes. Today, he struggled himself to hold it together. He was unconcerned about himself. It was his son, Jason that weighed heavy on his mind. He never told him much how proud of him he was and how much he loved him.

A rat squeaked and sheltered in the cell with the men. Ray shooed him away. "Go get out of here. Get back to your family," Ray whispered. His attention was drawn to outside. The sound of trucks splashing through the mud road. Ray climbed to his feet and peered through the bars. General Chow had returned. He climbed out of the armoured truck and watched his troops dismount from the two troop trucks. Chow glanced across at the prison hut. He grinned at Ray. He delighted in keeping prisoners and was looking forward to the fast approaching deadline.

*

Jason broke through the dense foliage and came across the prison camp. He crouched down and took in his surroundings. His eyes darted around the small buildings. His attention drawn to a hut with bars on the front.

"Dad," Jason said under his breath excitedly. He could see his father at the bars looking out. Jason's heart pounded. He wanted to shout out and run over. The child in him was pulling him forward. He longed to get a hug from his dad and show him that he made it this far alone. He took a deep breath and told himself to come up with a plan. He noticed the armed guards, and although he had a pistol, he knew he would be out numbered and out gunned.

He continued to take mental notes of where the guards came and went. He thought one small hut over a stream was used as a bathroom. The guards went in and left a few minutes later. The sleeping dorm and a larger building used for preparing food. There was one hut that was solitary. He was unsure what it was until he saw General Chow.

The third guard manned the lookout post twenty feet in the air. He used binoculars to check the perimeter. Most of the time he leant back and sucked on a cigarette.

The pirate looking guy from the motor launch, Jason said to himself as he watched General Chow. Jason studied the area, trying to come up with a plan. He sat back against a tree hidden in the undergrowth and slept on and off for a couple of hours until it was dark. He had less than twelve hours to do something before execution of the prisoners started.

He quietly made his way down to the stream that ran between the camp and waded in. He slowly walked into the camp, keeping low. He paused, buried his hands into mud on the bank, and covered his hair and face in the brown stodgy mess. He crept up to the largest wood and bamboo hut it was raised high off the ground to keep it dry when in severe rainstorms the stream matured into a river.

He crawled on the soggy ground and slithered underneath the hut. He could feel a leech on his forearm. Ignoring it he kept moving forward. He placed a Claymore mine under the hunt and slowly made his way back out, making sure he never pulled out the wires. Further up the stream, he placed another under a hut he suspected they used for cooking and supplies.

One guard sluggishly leant against a flagpole. The red communist flag flopped down and dripped water as if in submission. Jason put his equipment down and slowly made his way towards the guard. Pausing to concentrate, he built up an adrenaline rush inside his system. His pupils darkened and his heartbeat raced. He blocked out every sound around him and focused on the unsuspecting guard. He crept forward on his toes behind his prey like a lion ready to pounce. Every muscle fiber in his agile body was fully wound and alert, ready to spring into action.

He knew he had to be quick. One sound from the guard would alert the whole prison. Jason came up behind the guard and tapped him on the shoulder. As the guard turned, he pulled his right fist back, threw it forward and, just before impact, threw his shoulder into the blow. He struck the guards windpipe. The ferocious blow smashed the guard's trachea. He tried to gasp for air, but Jason unleashed a second blow to the poor man's nose. It was ferocious enough to knock him out cold.

Jason picked up the guard's gun and moved to his next victim. This guard was sleeping in a chair outside the general's hut. Jason slowly approached along the wooden walkway. Below, the stream cascaded smothering the light sound of his footsteps. Jason thought it would be a perfect place to lower his unconscious body.

"Oi!" shouted the startled guard clambering for his rifle. Jason launched into a kick and struck his face with his right foot. He had been taken by surprise as much as the guard. He thought the man was sleeping. "Giúp!" The guard screamed for help as he fell back, clutching his injured face.

"Shut it." Jason cursed. He pounced on the man and threw four punches into his face. Another shout came from up in the lookout post. The guard on lookout duty turned on the spot light. It shone around and soon found the injured guard with Jason pounding him.

A shot rang out, narrowly missing Jason. The whole camp came alive. Jason cursed to himself. His plan had gone disastrously wrong. He pulled the pin from a grenade, jumped up, and threw it up at the lookout post. It exploded and blew it apart. The guard fell with the wreckage.

The prisoners woke and peered out of the bars. "It's a rescue party," one shouted excitedly.

Jason dived back down to the stream, found the switch, and set off the Claymore mines. The explosion tore apart the sleeping quarters. Two of General Chow's men had got clear. They ran towards Jason shirtless, carrying rifles waist height, and shooting at anything that moved.

"Look! Ione of ours down there by the stream," Marcel Deschamps said, pointing at Jason. "He looks French, but small." The others looked as Jason rose and opened fire with his pistol in his right hand, shooting at the oncoming guards. With his left hand, he tossed a grenade. "God he's young, looks like a kid."

The words *looks like a kid* hit Ray like an atom bomb going off in his head. Ray's heart pounded as he pushed past the others and forced his head tight between the bars for a closer look, deep inside he was desperate. Could it be that it was the one person in the world he loved?

The prisoners looked in the direction of the explosions. A huge ball of flames shot across the compound. They could just make out the image of someone running fast along bamboo the walkway. A guard stood in his way and raised his gun. The runner jumped into the air in a flying karate kick and took him out.

"Wow did you see that?" Marcel shouted.

“Look at that little guy go.”

As Ray watched, he could hardly believe his eyes. “It’s Jason,” he cried. Tears streamed down his face as he proudly watched his son sprinting towards General Chow's hut. The grenade exploded. The two men in pursuit were blown several feet up into the air. Fire had broken out in most parts of the camp and illuminated the whole complex.

From out of nowhere, a soldier ran towards Jason, swinging wildly with a sword. Jason skidded and slid below the sword and took the sword-wielding soldiers feet away. The man's legs were sent up in the air. Before he landed, Jason pulled his victims arm over his shoulder and, in a classic Judo move, threw him. The sword pinned the man down into the ground through his chest. Another soldier ran towards Jason shooting his rifle. Jason dove into the stream and went under.

For a few moments he was gone. Ray looked on, terrified that his son had just been hit. The guard searched the area, prodding the long grass with his rifle. An ear-piercing scream broke the temporary silence. Jason had sprung up from under the water and hit the man between the legs with all his power. It caused a vascular rupture on the man's reproductive parts. He whimpered and collapsed in severe pain.

“Ouch, I bet that hurt.” Carl Bradley, the American journalist, grimaced. “That guy looks young. He’s got to be a US Navy Seal. They seem to be getting younger or I’m just getting old.”

"No, he must be a French Legionnaire. Look at him go," Marcel said. "We have been rescued by the French. *Vive La France*! That guys amazing."

General Chow aimed and shot his rifle at Jason. The bullet hit the ground near his foot. The mud splashed up and hit Jason. He ran forward crouching and keeping low. In this position, Chow could not see him for a good shot. He had to move further into the open by the bank of the stream.

Chow paused. The boy was gone. He shot several shots into the water and cursed. He kept firing until he had unloaded his rifle, still cursing and screaming and calling Jason a half-breed. Chow's attention was drawn to the prisoners who looked on. In anger, he fired at them before realizing his rifle was empty. He cursed again and threw the rifle at the prisoners. He took out his revolver and took aim.

Ray and the others looked horrified. They had no protection from the insane general. Jason appeared from behind a burning hut and ran towards the general. He leapt into the air in a flying kick and caught General Chow's arm. Both fell to the ground. The revolver span towards the stream.

Both Jason and the general sprang to their feet. The general pulled out his dagger and circled Jason, like a fox preparing to move in on his prey. Ray took a deep breath. He gripped with all his strength at the bars, trying in vain to break them. He felt helpless watching his son being circled by the knife-wielding madman.

Jason concentrated on the general. He waited for the man to make his attack. When he did, Jason sprang clear and caught the hand holding the knife with both hands and twisted. He pulled down, threw up his knee into the general's chest ,and threw the general over his shoulder.

A solider fired a warning shot in Jason's direction, but safe enough away, concerned he may hit the General. Jason, still holding the general' arm, twisted it further until he dropped his knife. Jason scooped it up and threw it at the solider. It span at terrific speed through the air and caught his arm, not doing enough damage to stop him, but it gave Jason enough time to take out his pistol and fire three shots. Two hit the soldier. The man fell back and tumbled down to the stream.

Another soldier was running towards Jason with a rifle and bayonet. He never got much closer before Jason unloaded his gun into the man's chest. Chow had recovered. He threw himself at Jason, screaming, trying to bite, kick. and hit him. Jason stepped back and blocked his attack. Another guard had recovered from the explosion. He ran to the general's aid.

Jason was attacked from both sides. He hopped onto his right foot and unleashed his left foot. It sprung out like a piston and hit the general in the face, breaking his nose Jason stepped forward and threw his right fist into the man's rib cage. He followed with six more to the man's face before spinning and throwing a waist height kick into the man's face. The powerful blow knocked him out and several feet across the stream.

Another guard attacked him with a sword. Jason ducked, threw himself forward, and caught the man's wrist holding the sword. In a single swift move, he bent the man's wrist back and forced the sword back onto the guard. Jason kicked the guard's legs away, causing him to fall on his own sword. Not content with that, Jason span on his right leg and threw a left footed Mae Geri kick at the fallen man on his knees that knocked him across the walkway facedown with the sword stuck threw his back.

Jason paused for breath. He knelt down, taking in his surroundings and noticed the general had gone. His eyes darted around the complex for any more soldiers. For now, it was clear. He ran towards the prison hut and started to cut through the ropes holding the bamboo together. He passed the knife inside. The men were stronger than him. They soon cut their way out. Rather than let them out, Jason squeezed through the gap and ran to his father.

"Dad," Jason cried as he hugged his father. Ray clutched his son tight and nuzzled his face into his son's neck. The others watched in amazement. Jason turned to the others. "We have to move. There are soldiers everywhere. Pick up some guns on the way out of the camp. Follow me."

They all squeezed through the opening and followed Jason. He ran in a crouching position, pointing at guns to be picked up as they passed . Ray stuck close behind his son. They followed Jason for twenty minutes before he stopped and took out his compass to get his bearings. He gave his gun to his father. “Here, you take it. I’m a lousy shot.” He gave him his supply of bullets and looked back at the map. “This way. We're going southeast. We'll take the river and travel down towards the China Sea.

“When are we meeting up with the others?” Marcel asked.

Jason looked at him and, in a typical Steed fashion, raised his eyebrows. “Others? What others?”

“The Americans, British, or French or was it a joint effort that rescued us?” Marcel asked in his strong French accent.

“No others. Just us now. Come on, we have to move,” Jason said turning to move.

Ray caught his son’s shoulder. “Jason, where are the troops? That’s what he meant. When and where are we meeting up with them?” Ray asked. lovingly massaging his son’s shoulder.

“It’s just me, Dad. I had to do something. George Young said the governments couldn’t get involved so I kinda, em, snuck away.” Jason picked up on his father’s look. “I thought you would be pleased.”

Ray concealed his grin. “I am Jase, but isn’t there anyone else helping you? Are we completely on our own out here?”

“Yes. But I have a plan. We can travel along

the river. We may find a boat or launch, get to the coast, and then try and contact your ship."

The men stood around in a group looking down at Jason. He felt slightly uncomfortable with the situation. He looked at his father and shrugged his shoulders.

"Let me get this straight. You and you alone did all that?" Marcel asked.

Jason nodded.

"How did you get here son?" Carl asked.

"I hid on a aircraft, got to Thailand, and borrowed a small plane. I had to crash-land it on a Vietnamese beach. They were going to shoot me down. I did the rest on foot or boat. The locals think I'm Amerasian so I can get around okay. A local orphanage near here gave me food. The kids had a collection of weapons I used. They find them in the Jungle."

Ray stroked his son's blond hair. "Will you ever learn to let others take care of adult problems? You should be at school, not out here getting shot at and blowing up buildings, not to mention armed guards."

"But Dad! They were gonna do nothing everyone was thinking *someone* must do something so I thought, well I'm *someone* and here I am."

"Then young man, we owe you a big thank you. But for now we had better come up with a plan to get out," Marcel said. He took the map from Jason. "Where are we exactly?"

Jason showed him on the map. "Here. We can follow the river. We'll have plenty of water, food, and maybe find a boat. It's about forty miles," Jason said.

They watched as he pointed with his fingers across the map. Marcel placed his huge finger next to Jason's. It made Jason's hand look smaller than they were for a twelve-year-old.

"Why don't we just travel west to Cambodia? It's ten to twelve miles. We could do that in a day. It makes much more sense it will be safer. We go west. If we move fast we could do it before tomorrow night," Marcel said.

"No, they would be expecting that. Wong Tong says to defeat your opponent you must do the opposite to what he thinks. We must go southeast. They would never think we would do that because it's farther, harder going, and more dangerous. We have to travel through Ho Chi Minh City, but if we do it at night on the river, we should get through right under their noses."

"Who the hell is Wong Tong?" Carl asked.

Ray looked at him. "Probably better not to ask." Ray said.

"Well, he's your son."

"Trust me, it won't help," Ray said. He

looked at Jason. “Marcel has got a good point son, it will be quicker. You did a great job getting us out, but these guys are all military trained. Let them take some of the load now.”

“No, that’s dumb. We know the Vietcong are going to be after you. Where do you think they are going to look? We go southeast.” Jason did not try to conceal his exasperation. He folded up his map and tucked his compass in is shirt pocket. He started walking ahead and stopped when he realized no one was following.

“Maybe we should split up,” Marcel suggested. “They will try and track us, but we should go west, it’s so much quicker.”

They all discussed it for a few minutes. Jason stood away, impatiently tapping his foot with his arms folded. When they finished talking Ray strolled over to Jason.

“We are all going West, Jason. It’s quicker and safer. It’s too dangerous to try and go through the city. Besides, it’s almost thirty miles farther. These men are tired and hungry,” Ray said. He went to put his hand on Jason’s shoulder, but Jason pulled away.

Jason cursed. “Let the bloody French and journalists go west. I came here to get you, not them. Dad, I always trust my instincts. It has saved my life before and others. Wong Tong said always—” He was interrupted.

“Yes son I have heard all Wong Tongs

sayings. You quote them enough. Wouldn't you rather be out of this jungle by tomorrow?"

"Derrr of course I would. I stink of sweat, my feet are rubbed raw, the mosquitoes and leeches think I'm Christmas dinner, I'm hot, tired, and hungry."

"Well then—" Ray said.

"But I'm also alive and so are you. I know it would be easy to go west but if it was that easy, the Americans would have won the war here. Dad, I beg of you. Please come southeast. Let the others try west. I hope they make it, but I know it will be safer this way." Jason moved forward and held his father's hands. "Dad I'm right about this."

Ray stared into his sons sapphire blue eyes and nodded.

"There is a large barge slightly North of here, em but it's got no engine," Jason said trying to suggest something. He noticed his father's disappointed expression. "Yeah that won't help, will it? But I'm right about going South, Dad."

Ray looked at the others. They were waiting for his answer. "Marcel is right. It would be better if we split up into two teams. We will all go west. It will be quicker and easier."

Marcel took four others. The three British crew stayed with Ray. Jason was furious with his father. He was physically shaking in anger. He felt like he was being treated like a child. They said their

goodbyes and watched Marcel leave. Ray told him they would travel half a mile north before heading west.

Chapter Twenty-Three

Jason sat on a tree stump, watching as Marcel and his team left. They saluted him. He reluctantly returned the salute and nodded when they thanked him and said goodbye. Ray introduced Jason to the British team. Cookie was from Glasgow, Scotland. He was thin but tall, just over six foot six. He was originally a member of the 1st battalion Scots Guard. Every other word he spoke was a curse word. Jason liked him. He made him laugh.

Then there was Evans from Wales. He was average height and weight. Most of the time he was humming a tune to himself. The third British member was Jack from Yorkshire. He had an acne-scarred face. Extremely thin and wiry with short blond hair. He was missing the little finger on his right hand. He told Jason he lost it in a card game. Jason never understood if it was a joke or he was serious.

Ray asked Jason for the map and compass. Jason threw it at him. He was still angry with his father for wanting to go west. Ray had everyone join them. He used the gun as a pointer.

"Okay, guys. we have a long journey. We are here and we need to get to here." He pointed down the river to the east coast.

"But, sir. You told Marcel you agreed with him and said we would be going west," Jack said.

Jason watched, not sure what his father was planning.

"Jason's right. It will be safer to go Southeast, hard going yes, but safer. If Marcel gets caught and tortured and asked what way we went, what is he going to tell them?" Ray asked.

"Genius, Sir. I can see why you're a Lieutenant now," Evans said.

Jason beamed; Ray looked at him and winked.

Ray went first. He had heard that local people were getting injured or maimed from land mines left over after the war. Like any father, he felt protective. Jason was relegated to following him The other three followed closely behind. Apart from Jason, they carried a gun each and the little ammunition they picked up.

They emerged one by one from the jungle. They sat and bent over, drenched in sweat and rain. It had only taken an hour to reach the river. They drank from the dirty water, pushing away the bugs that swam on the surface first. Jason plunged his head under to wash off the sweat and all the dead mosquitoes he squashed on his face and neck. "Hey young'un drinking that water will give you the squirts it will," Cookie said in his broad Scottish accent.

Jason wiped his mouth. "So? You will get the squirts too." Jason grinned.

"Nah, I'm Scottish. Unlike you Southern softies, we're born standing up with boots on," Cookie joked.

"My mum was Scottish. My grandparents live near Glasgow."

"Och aye that explains how you are so tough and rescued us. You were incredible back there. You kicked the stuffing out of them." Cookie grinned.

Jason studied his knuckles; they were cut and had bled after his fights with the guards. "My skin's not so tough. My knuckles always split open when I hit someone hard."

Cookie glanced over and laughed. "Aye that a be the English in ya. You can blame your father for your soft skin, laddie."

Jason laughed. He took an instant liking to Cookie. He looked up at his father. "Dad, it's your fault my knuckles always split."

Ray glanced up from the map. He waved his hand to swipe away a fly and continued looking at the map. Jason felt strangely relaxed. He knew they were still in great danger but with his father next to him, he felt at ease. He was enjoying spending time with him and the others. The dangers seemed to have vanished now he was here with his father and the three British troops.

Ray watched his son laughing and joking with Cookie. Seeing his son laugh made him smile. It was the side of Jason he loved. The part he witnessed earlier at the prison camp disturbed Ray. He was, on one hand, proud of the way his son took on all the guards but, on the other hand, he was unsure if the physical attacks on people and death that Jason had witnessed at such a young age would cause emotional scars for him later in life.

Cookie washed his large arms in the water. and Jason noticed his tattoos. One portrayed a pin-up girl, another with the Scottish flag and the words 'Mum' underneath. "Did they hurt when you had them?" Jason asked.

"Eye. I would be lying if I said no, but it was worth it. Will you get some when you're older?" Cookie asked.

"No, tattoos are just images or words like bumper stickers. And you wouldn't put bumper stickers on a Rolls Royce." Jason laughed, flexing his small biceps.

Chapter Twenty-Four

With a bandaged, broken nose, General Chow screamed down a radio and called in reinforcements. The Vietnamese government was furious with the escape. They told General Chow that on no account were the prisoners to leave Vietnam. He must capture them or kill them. They gave him a battalion of just over six hundred troops complete with seven helicopter gunships. The first order of priority was to seal the border between Vietnam and Cambodia.

His troops were flown in and settled on the Cambodia border. From here, they started moving west. Scouts were sent out to look for the prisoners; sniffer dogs were flown into the camp in an attempt to track the prisoners. General Chow was leaving nothing to chance. He wanted them all captured, dead or alive. He also gave a description of the Amerasian boy; he wanted him alive if possible so he could deal with him personally.

A villager from the small village outside Tay Ninh gave information that the boy with blond hair and blue eyes was seen at the orphanage and left just before the troops arrived. In retaliation, the whole village was burnt to the ground. General Chow's men searched for the children and Claudette. They had gone into hiding in retaliation the Vietcong bombed the area. A few villagers were found but Claudette and the children were not seen.

The smoke and flames from the burning village could be seen for miles around. General Chow was pleased and was certain the Amerasian children would not have survived.

*

Evans whistled a signal; he was farther ahead along the riverbank where a small boat carrying supplies made its way up river. He let it pass so it was between him and the others.

"We need it to get down river," Jason whispered to his father.

"It's got three men on it. We have to lie low. If they see us, they will flee and give us away. They may even have a radio," Ray said. Jason peered through the long grass. "Jason, keep down. It's too risky."

"They won't be alarmed if they see me," He argued and picked up his father's rifle. He walked into the river up to his waist, holding the rifle above his head.

"Hey," he shouted, waving his arms. "Hey." They looked over at the boy. The boat engine slowed. They shouted back something in Vietnamese and turned towards him. Jason held the rifle with one hand above his head and held his other hand out for money. The boatmen assumed the Amerasian boy had found a gun he wanted to sell. They knew it would fetch several hundred Vietnamese dong and they could probably get it cheap from the boy

“What’s he doing?” Jack asked.

“He’s getting us a ride.” Ray sighed. He was unsure if he should be furious with Jason for doing the opposite of what he had said or happy with his help.

Jason waded out to the motorboat. They were asking him questions in Vietnamese. He just smiled and kept shaking the rifle above his head like it was a grand prize. They took his hand and lifted him in the boat. He rubbed a finger and thumb together. The universal symbol for money.

"Con lai." The older man laughed and tried to push Jason off the boat. Jason noticed he had just one tooth in his mouth and that was a dark brown color. It reminded him of Bugs Bunny. Ray looked on concerned. He took Jack's rifle and aimed it at the man in case Jason needed help.

“Hey, less of the half-breed talk, Bugs,” Jason said, standing his ground.

The older one toothed man swung the rifle butt towards Jason and shouted, "Con lai."

“I was going to be nice,” Jason said after he ducked. He leapt up and threw a roundhouse, kicking at the man knocking him back into the water. "Hope you can swim, Bugs." He caught the rifle before the man splashed into the river and quickly turned it on his two-crew members. They both raised their hands. The old man struggled and climbed back on board his boat, cursing under his breath. Jason turned to the riverbank at his father.

"We got a boat." Jason grinned.

Ray, Cookie, and Jack waded out to the boat and climbed on board.

"So, what would you do with these if I wasn't here?" Ray asked his son, looking at the boatmen.

Jason passed the rifle back to his father and shrugged his shoulders. "Em, probably just let them go later somewhere safe."

Ray raised his eyebrows and nodded. "Good. I was worried you would say kill them."

"No, they've done nothing wrong. Although Bugs here tried to keep the rifle without paying for it, and he's a racist."

"*Bugs*?" Cookie asked with a wide grin.

"Yeah wait until you see him open his mouth." Jason grinned.

"Racist?" Ray asked.

"Yeah, they call me Con Lai. That means half-breed. They think I'm Amerasian. I met quite a few of the kids here. Their fathers were American."

Jason said.

"American fathers?" Cookie asked.

"Yeah, well I guess the American troops were, em, you know, the birds and the bees stuff with the Vietnamese ladies and now there are thousands of kids here. Some are black, some red heads, and I saw one with blond hair. It's sad they get shouted at and spat on all the time and called Con Lai. Most of the families don't want them. They can't go to America. Many don't know their fathers or the father died and his family don't know they have a grandchild. Bit of a mess. Then you get idiots like Bugs here trying to steal from one and calling them Con Lai."

Jack worked out how to operate the boat. Ray told him to head down river. Cookie tied the boatmen up. He tied the rope a little too tight around the old man Jason called Bugs. He yelped. When he did, Cookie noticed his one brown tooth in the front of his mouth. It made Cookie laugh.

"War. Huh." Cookie sang in a loud deep voice. "What is it good for?"

"Absolutely nothing" Evans and Jack sang back in harmony.

"Say it again, y'all. War. Huh. What is it good for?" Cookie sang.

They continued to sing the song.. Jason had heard the Edwin Starr song on the radio before. He loved hearing Cookie and the others sing it.

Although they were service men, they enjoyed being part of the United Nations team that helped casualties of the war. The song was like an anthem to them.

*

Marcel and his group's location was discovered by General Chow's troops. A small battle erupted. The lack of firepower and sheer numbers of the Vietnamese killed Marcel. The Frenchman went down after a heroic fight. So did his men and the journalists. None of them survived. General Chow was delighted with the news; he ordered them to continue to search for the others and of course the boy, who he was now obsessed about and wanted dead or alive.

*

They had travelled just over two miles downstream. The river widened. Ray noticed a small island in the center. It was no more than twenty feet long with just a few trees on it but perfect for dropping off the boatmen. They tied the men to the trees and gagged them. It was getting dark, so they hoped it would be at least the next morning before they were seen by a passing fishing boat. By that time, Ray and his small team would be eight or nine hours away.

*

The Vietnamese government displayed pictures of the dead bodies to the world's media. The news broke all over the world. Scott watched the newsbreak on Television but gave a sigh of relief when he never heard Raymond Steed's name. The British still held out some hope. The only news they had is that the nine remaining prisoners had somehow escaped. Of those, five had been killed in a deadly shoot out. The British prisoners had yet to be located.

The motorboat they had taken was an old American patrol boat built especially for the Vietnam War. It didn't have a propeller. Instead, it used a high power water jet to propel itself along the river. This was so it would not get tangled up in weeds and could operate in shallow water. When the Americans left, many were stripped of the guns and used by fisherman or, in this case, boatmen to ferry fruit such as mangos up and down the river.

Ray sat on the boat's bench seat eating some bananas. He was soon joined by Jason. Within a few minutes, Jason had stretched out on the length of the bench and fallen asleep. He used his father's lap as a pillow. Ray gently parted Jason's blond hair and studied his son. Soft delicate skin, small lips and nostrils. He looked just like any other young boy asleep. A different picture of what Ray had witnessed at the prison camp when he rescued them.

Evans, Jack, and Cookie each took a turn driving for a few hours. It was difficult navigating at night. The food and fresh water on the boat carried came as a welcome relief.

Morning broke, and birds started a dawn

chorus of singing. The sun lifted itself up from the horizon of trees as if it had been nesting among them. Jason stretched. His father had moved and put a jacket under Jason's head and covered him in a blanket. Jason popped his head up and looked at the riverbank. They were getting close to Ho Chi Min City. A few small homes were scattered along the riverbank on both sides. They encountered a few fishing boats but nothing else.

Jason jumped up and took in his surroundings. "We are near Ho Chi Min City." Cookie smiled. Ray, Jack, and Evans were all asleep on the deck of the boat.

"Get down," Jason said. He took the boats controls. "You stand out. Keep down. You should have woken me earlier before we got to the populated area."

"Och its fine laddie. I'm just a guy driving a boat," Cookie said. Ray and the others woke up.

"No, you're a westerner," Jason said.

"And who the bloody hell are you? Foo Man Cho? You are just as much a westerner as me. Actually, more so with your blond hair and baby blue eyes." Cookie belched.

"No, they think I'm Amerasian. I won't be suspected," Jason said. "Keep down all of you."

"I need a pee," Jack said.

"Hold it. Jason's right; we could get seen.

Let's just get passed the city without being stopped," Ray said.

It started to rain; Jason picked up a folded red communist flag and made a bandana out of it. It solved the purpose of keeping the constant heavy rain off his head and covered his blond hair.

The farther they travelled, the more built up the riverbank became. Jason had to slow the boat down a little. He noticed most of the other boats went at a slow pace. The river was crowded in a few spots with fisherman and water taxis. The city was packed. Over three million people. made it their home. Jason thought the heavy rain would mean less chance of being stopped.

"We need fuel." Evans said. He had poured the last can of diesel into the tank. He joined Ray and the others who were sat on the floor keeping low.

Ray looked up at Jason. "Jase we need fuel. See if you can see some," Ray said. Jason nodded. He looked around but was unsure how he could find fuel.

*

US President Ford and Vice President Rockefeller held another meeting with the security chiefs. It included the Australian Prime Minister and the British Foreign secretary. Max Fisher was to chair the meeting again. As soon as they all arrived Max took to the floor and addressed everyone.

"I'm sure, gentlemen that you all watched the news reports. Five men have been killed while trying to escape. We still have some people in Vietnam loyal to us. They are technically agents deep in enemy territory. They informed us that all nine prisoners escaped. The prison was partially destroyed, and several North Vietnamese soldiers were killed and injured. We are still unsure of the whereabouts of the British men. No bodies have been found. We can only assume they escaped." Fisher stopped and took a drink of water to clear his throat. "Also, a small village outside Tay Ninh has been burnt to the ground and bombed. Our informant told us that a blond haired, blue-eyed boy was previously hiding at an Amerasian orphanage. The Vietcong destroyed the village in retaliation. The children have not been seen since, suspected killed."

"That's very sad. Although I don't really believe all this Amerasian children nonsense, just a bunch of Vietnamese refugees wanting a green card. Back to the prisoners. Do we know how they escaped exactly?" President Ford asked.

"No sir, although our informant at the hospital told us one man was seriously injured, but was not shot or cut," Fisher said.

"Meaning, what exactly?" President Ford asked.

"Meaning that it was the work of someone highly skilled in martial arts."

"How many Vietnamese were killed on the

escape?" Vice President Rockefeller asked.

"Reports say nine dead, six injured. Two of those are serious," Fisher said.

"Gentlemen. One has spoken to my people who have worked with this Jason Steed chap, If this was his doing expect the body count to increase," British Defence Secretary Roy Mason warned. His eyebrows danced as if floating over his head. "He has a viscous temper that he can't control. He's a lethal weapon. Two years ago he won the under sixteen Karate Championship when he was only ten. He has mastered other forms and has been trained to kill a man with a single blow. From what I have heard, his speed and reflexes are extraordinary."

"He's still a twelve-year-old boy, and we still don't yet know if it was him that broke them out of the prison camp," Fisher argued.

"But you can come up with no other explanation either?" President Ford suggested. "Then, if we assume they are still on the run, what's your plan to get them out?"

"We don't have a plan. We have to wait. Raymond Steed is a decorated British Naval officer. He must be in charge now. Although he has no combat experience, his son however... well I think we have all read the reports on him now. We will monitor all radio frequencies and let them come to us." Fisher paused. "Unless we can send in a crack squad to help them?"

"No one steps foot on Vietnam. Jason Steed

is working alone. So far he has stowed away on a US aircraft, assaulted a guard at a US base, and stolen a small aircraft that the US army was guarding. If he is responsible and gets caught, we have to distance ourselves," President Ford said. "Although my thoughts and prayers are with him and the prisoners."

Chapter Twenty-Five

Jason noticed a small wooden dock, it had a small boat tied alongside it. On the dock itself was some jerry cans. He hoped they contained fuel.

"I can see a boat dock. Keep down, we may be able to get some fuel," Jason said. He threw a tarpaulin over his father and the others. Jack made a peephole with his knife.

He slowed the boat down and pulled up to the dock faster than he intended. It collided with a loud thump and made it rock.

"Oops," Jason said, biting his bottom lip. An angry man limped out of a small hut at the other end of the dock, shouting at Jason. The dock was like a small pier jetting out into the river, no more than twenty feet in length. It had some wooden slats missing that had to be stepped over. Jason thought it would probably fall to bits in a good storm. The collision with his boat couldn't have helped much.

Jason jumped onto the dock and took a rope from the front of the boat and tied it to a wooden support. The man approached him and, despite Jason's smile, was still just as angry.

"I need to buy fuel," Jason said in French, holding out the last of his US dollars. The limping man took the money and counted it. He had no idea what the boy had said but he seemed happy. He laughed and waved his hand at the fuel cans. Jason walked over to two of them and grabbed one in each hand. "Oh," he said when he realized they were too heavy to lift one in each hand. He managed one at a time. He struggled to lift it across to the boat. "That's all right, you guys just relax and let me do all the work." He puffed to the men hiding under the tarpaulin.

As he returned to get the second one he noticed the man with the limp talking to a soldier. He looked at Jason and slowly walked down the small wooden boat dock. Jason hurried and picked up the second can. He carried it back to the boat. The solider lit a cigarette and asked Jason a question in Vietnamese.

Jason nodded and smiled and continued what he was doing. When he tried to untie the boat the soldier asked the question again.

"Parlez-vous français?" Jason asked if he spoke French. He was surprised and relieved when the solider replied 'yes.'

"What is the fuel for?" The soldier asked.

"The boat. I have to get back to my mother with the boat," Jason said. He fidgeted nervously.

"Have you bought fuel for your boat before?" the guard asked.

Jason thought he was smirking. “Yes. I always buy fuel for my mother's boat.” Jason said.

“Really? But this is petrol.” he said.

“Yes.” Jason said, unsure why he was asking the questions. “Your French is good,” Jason said trying to change the subject.

The soldier took a step onto the boat. He took his rifle down that was slung over his shoulder. “Your boat runs on diesel not petrol. You are either a stupid half breed or you’re lying to me.”

Jason was lost for words. “Em.” He paused. “I lied sir. I found some guns. I was going to sell them. They are hidden under here.” Jason pointed at the tarpaulin.

Becoming more excited. He threw his cigarette in the water and approached to lift the tarpaulin. Jason spun on his leg and threw a perfectly aimed kick at the soldier. His boot caught the man's stomach and threw him back onto the dock and over the over side into the water. Jason untied the boat and slammed it into reverse.

The soldier came up from the water shouting and screaming at Jason. His rifle was still on the dock. When the boat was far enough away to turn. He put it into forward gear and opened it up on full speed.

As they pulled away the wet solider started shooting. Immediately, the boat started spluttering. Ray and the others climbed out from under the tarpaulin.

"She's out of fuel son. I fill her up," Jack said picking up a Jerry can. The boat was far enough away not to get hit but the shooting had attracted more soldiers who were nearby.

"Um, I don't think that fuels any good It's petrol," Jason said sheepishly.

Ray looked at him. "Then why?" He stopped in mid sentence. The engine completely stopped. Cookie tried to start it but it would not fire up. "We're like sitting ducks out here." Jason stepped back. He watched his father and the others trying to restart the boat. He noticed a launch coming towards them full of soldiers. It was a Vietnamese Naval armed river launch.

"We have to get off this and swim to shore. Look," Jason said, pointing at the approaching vessel.

Ray nodded at him. "He's right. We better make it quick."

"Give me your lighter," Jason said to Cookie, holding out his hand. He took the caps off the Jerry cans and kicked them over, spilling the fuel onto the deck. Once everyone had dived into the water, Jason lit the lighter, threw it at the fuel, and dived off the boat seconds before it erupted into flames.

The black smoke from the fire gave them sufficient cover to swim farther along the shore. The shoreline was packed with wooden and bamboo huts, most held together with rope and twine. They came to an uninhabited area of long grass and vegetation. It was not ideal, but they could hide in among it until they could find a way out.

"How was I to know it was a diesel boat?" Jason said. He felt he had let the others down.

"Och don't worry sonny, you didn't know." Cookie smiled.

*

General Chow had previously given orders to be given a full report on anything suspicious or any sightings of the boy with the blond hair. He was at a make shift camp over forty miles away looking for the British escapees. When he was given the news, he smiled in admiration of the British plan to go in the other direction. Immediately, he ordered his helicopter and flew to Ho Chi Min City. His troops arrived by the truckload. Motor launches were being called in along with more helicopters for the search.

The news of the search made it back to Max Fisher. It was frustrating for him knowing the prisoners and Jason had made it so far. The British aircraft carrier, HMS Hermes, was still in the China Sea, only fifty miles from the city.

*

They hid among the water reeds for nine hours until darkness descended. They had stayed still most of the day, apart from pulling leeches off themselves. Jason sat next to his father and rested his head on fathers arm. “Sorry, Dad. I tried.”

Ray stroked his son’s head. “I still can’t get use to you talking now. Your voice has broken.” He sighed. “Well, young warrior what would your Wong Tong say to do now?”

Jason smiled and gazed at his father. He had never shown an interest in his son’s karate and often regarded Wong Tong’s sayings as nonsense. “Well...” Jason said and paused. “To defeat the opponent, you must do the opposite of what they expect. So what would the Vietcong be expecting us to do now?”

Ray lovingly held his sons hand, raised it to his mouth, and kissed it. “Hmm, they would expect us to hide out for a few days and try and carry on down river,” he said.

“So, that means we have to swim back were we came from immediately. Let’s go back to the boat dock and steal a Vietnamese naval boat. You should know how to control it,” Jason said.

“Are you crazy? Did you bump your head son? The place is swarming with soldiers and helicopters looking for us,” Ray said just as another helicopter flew over, its large searchlight brightening up the area.

“Yes, they are searching here, up and down the river, but not where we came from. They will expect us to lay low for a while. Let's go right now and steal a boat,” Jason said.

Ray studied his son. The searchlight broke

through the mango tree they hid under, lighting up his sons adorable face. His blond hair was stuck up in all directions. His face was tanned, dirty with mosquitoes bites on his cheeks. "If you feel it's our best option okay, but if we don't make it..." Ray paused; he wrapped his arm around his son and squeezed him tight. "I have to tell you, when I saw you taking down those guards back at the prison, standing there watching my son, was the proudest moment of my life. If I get killed tonight I will die a proud man, a very, very proud man. I love you, Jason," Ray croaked. His body shook as he fought with his emotions.

It was the first time Jason had ever seen his father show real emotion. He was shocked and a little teary eyed himself.

Jason dug his fingers into the mud and came up with two fistfuls of black sticky mud. "Dad," He whispered. Ray turned and looked at his son. Jason splattered his father's face with the gooey mess. "We need camouflage," he sniggered.

The four men, all with blackened faces, crept back into the water behind Jason. They gently swam towards the naval launches.

"This is bloody suicide," Evans hissed.

"War. Huh," Cookie sang in a low deep voice. "What is it good for?"

"Absolutely nothing," Evans and Jack sang back in harmony.

"Say it again, y'all," Cookie sang.

"Shush." Ray ordered.

Jason looked back and grinned at Cookie.

*

Three Vietcong naval motor launches were moored at the dock. A fourth launch arrived, it's bright searchlights lit up the area. A few hundred yards away a helicopter was landing in a clearing. The whole area was alive with troops coming and going in their search for the escape prisoners.

General Chow stepped out of the helicopter; he adjusted his eye patch before he saluted a fellow officer. He stood stiffly upright with his hands behind his back and raised himself on his toes and slowly turned his head, his watchful eye capturing everything around him. He barked orders and marched towards the Vietcong new headquarters in Cho Minh City. It had previously been a hotel, but since the defeat of the South Vietnamese and the Americans, it had been taken over.

Chapter Twenty-Six

The small group gently swam to the side of the fourth motor launch. The men could just stand with their noses clear of the water. Cookie was able to stand flat-footed while Ray, Jack, and Evans all stood on tiptoe. Cookie reached and held Jason under his arms so he could rest like the others. The four of them caught their breaths and listened, trying to hear how many men were on the boat.

"Lift me up," Jason whispered to Cookie. He raised him high enough to catch both hands on the side of the boat. Jason's fingers curled around the rim of the boat. He pulled his lightweight body up and peaked on the deck. A solitary solider sat on a bench seat watching the activities in the city and the comings and goings of the army. He felt lucky to be given an easy job of watching the boat. He was safe out here. He remembered a time when the Americans were here and before that the French. Now was a much safer time. They could relax, maybe even get some leave and go back up to North Vietnam and see his family.

He pulled a cigarette out of his top pocket and struck a match. He inhaled deeply savouring the strong nicotine. He felt a hand grab his mouth and pull him back onto the floor of the boat. The hand was wet, smooth, and small, like that of a woman, he thought. He felt another hand squeezing the side of his neck. It stung. He struggled and tried to scream or get the hand from his mouth and the hand squeezing his carotid artery on his neck. He felt light headed. Dazed, he lost his strength. The grip continued until he was unconscious.

Jason held his grip on the man's neck for just a few seconds longer. He wanted to be sure he was out cold. With his father here, Jason wanted to impress. He didn't want the solider coming around and raising the alarm. Just a few more seconds should do it he told himself. He thought back to when Wong Tong had taught him the hold. 'Not too long,' Wong Tong had said, else they won't recover.

He released his grip and crawled back to the side of the boat and peered over. "Okay, you can come up," Jason whispered to the others.

As Cookie was the tallest the others used him as a ladder, gaining enough height to climb up onto the boat. Ray was first up. He nodded at Jason with approval. Jack and Evans both climbed up. They bent down and, together pulled Cookie up. Jason went back to the soldier and felt his pulse, nothing. Thinking he was feeling in the wrong place, he tried again and nothing.

Ray was busying himself with the boat controls. Evans checked the fuel. The boat carried a mounted machine gun on the front. It was loaded with a belt of bullets and more were stored in boxes next to it. He looked down at Jason and had to take a double look. He was performing CPR on the soldier.

"What are you doing?" Ray asked.

"He's got no pulse. I think I killed him. I didn't mean too," Jason said thumping the man's chest.

Evans crawled over and felt his pulse. He nodded at Jason. "He's dead, boyo. Nothing you can do for him now," Evans said.

Jason sat back on the floor, looking at the dead soldier horrified. "I never meant to kill him, " he said in a whisper. He looked at his hands and rubbed them on his pants, trying to rid the feel of the man from them.

"It was him or us Jason," Cookie said. "You did well to take him down without him raising the alarm. You saved all of us. Don't beat yourself up over killing him, laddie. It's a very fine line between knocking someone out and killing them. He was a soldier and this is war and remember, what's it good for?"

"Absolutely nothing," Jason grimly said.

Ray picked up the dead man's helmet and placed it on his own head to try and hide his western features. The others kept down. He started the engine. Immediately, the boat's searchlight came on. Cookie pointed it at the shore. He hoped it would blind anyone who looked out to see what boat was leaving.

The motorboat pulled away from the dock. Ray kept it going back far enough to get clear of the other boats. Once he was clear, he put it into forward and they headed south down the river towards the South China Sea. Jack threw the dead soldier overboard.

Jason picked up the radio microphone and tuned the frequency to 37.1FM. Ray watched him.

"Careful, Jase. You'll give our location away," Ray said.

Jason took a breath before broadcasting. He clicked the microphone on and off in a series of dots and dashes in Morse code. He knew Scott would translate it. Others would too, even the Vietcong, but only Scott would be able to decipher it. *This is carrot cake eater, heading from Santa's City to the Olympian God. Prepare enough cake for five, over.* He repeated the message again.

"Santa's City? Olympian God? I got the carrot cake eater bit, but none of the rest. Who on earth will understand that message?" His father asked.

"A certain mate of mine who will be tuning in to 37.1FM on his international ham radio, but probably no one else, especially the Vietcong." Jason grinned.

"Scott?" Ray asked. "And if you're wrong?"

"Then its Plan B." Jason shrugged.

*

Thousands of miles away, Scott Turner heard the message on his ham radio. He came crashing down the stairs to use the phone. His parents watched him as he dialled the phone. Scott glanced at them.

"Jason just sent me a message," he told them and waited for the call to be answered. Eventually, he was put through to George Young.

"Mr. Young, Jason just left a message over the radio. I need to talk to the admiralty urgently," Scott said excited.

George agreed. He spoke to the admiralty and, after a few minutes, Admiral Hollyingberry himself contacted Scott. He was stunned by the call and never expected to hear direct.

"Let me get this straight, you're Jason Steed's friend and contact? Mr. George Young also tells me that you are also the young man that broke Jason's code when he was in Jakarta," Admiral Hollyingberry asked.

"Yes, Sir. Jason and I are best mates," Scott said.

"Well, our intelligence heard a message that we think is from Jason but have no idea what it means. Olympian Gods and Santa's City. We do understand who the carrot cake eater is. He needs to come up with something original there."

"You are correct, Si., Jason is the carrot cake eater as he said in the message he's leaving Santa's City or in this case. Ho Chi Ming City. I guess that's the best Jason could come up with Ho Ho Ho, from Santa."

"Oh, I see but what's the Olympian God got to do with it?" Admiral Hollyingberry asked.

"Er derrrrr. Olympian God. There are twelve mythical Olympian Gods and one was called Hermes. I mentioned that to Jason once and he called me a nerd. I listen to naval broadcasts on my radio, so I know our aircraft carrier HMS Hermes is close to Ho Chi Ming City in Vietnam," Scott said.

"Yes, she's quite close."

"Well sir, maybe you should inform HMS Hermes to prepare cake for five people. That will be the four British escaped prisoners and Jason," Scott said

"Well done, young man. You have a future in intelligence. You and Jason make a great team." Admiral Hollyingberry thanked him and dropped the phone.

*

Generals Chow's men eventually discovered a launch was missing. he alarm was raised. General Chow was livid that the British had the nerve to steal one of his launches to escape right from under his nose.

Chapter Twenty-Seven

After three hours, the river widened and became a little choppy. They were finally at the mouth of the river and entering the South China Sea.

"Dad, do you think Scott heard my message and passed it on?"

"I don't know. I hope so, but if the Vietcong pick it up we could be inviting trouble. We don't have enough fuel to get to Malaysia," Ray said.

"Looks like we have trouble," Cookie shouted pointing behind them.

They looked back. Three naval launches gave chase supported by two Helicopter gunships. Ray pushed the throttle forward to full speed. Cookie climbed onto the front of the boat to man the machine gun. Jack passed Evans and Ray both a rifle. Jason went into the wheelhouse and held the wheel. He looked up. The helicopter seemed to fly from the core of the sun.

"I doubt we can out run them. Those two look newer than this one. They may be faster." Ray said. "We're almost in the South China Sea. Another mile or so and we will be in international waters, although I doubt that will stop them. I hope Scott got your message, Jason, else we are in deep trouble."

The closet helicopter rapidly caught up and opened fire on the boat. Cookie shot back, sending dozens of bullets at the flying target. Ray, Jack, and Evans took their time aiming at the cockpit. A string of bullets pounded the water's surface and drew a line down the center of the boat. Evans screamed and held his arm. He fell onto his knees and groaned. Blood oozed through his fingers holding his wound.

Jason ripped off his shirt and tied it tightly around Evans's wound. Smoke started billowing from under the floorboards. The engine started to make a rasping sound. The helicopter turned to take a second run. Cookie took aim and fired the machine gun at it. Ray and Jack took aim, the three of them franticly trying to hit it as it approached. Being shot at by helicopter brought back terrible memories for Jason. It was how the Jakarta massacre started.

The helicopter exploded in midair; a huge ball of flames filled the sky. Burning debris rained down from the smoke filled sky. Jason could feel the heat on his face as he looked up.

"Let that be a bloody lesson to ya," Cookie shouted. Ray went back into the wheelhouse and picked up the microphone from the radio. He turned the transmitter into 30.99FM, the Royal Navy's emergency radio frequency.

"Requesting immediate assistance. South China Sea, Ho Chi Ming estuary. This is lieutenant Raymond Steed, Royal Navy, over." Ray repeated the message.

"Lieutenant Steed. This is HMS Hermes. We are three miles Northeast of you, over."

Ray was surprised how close the Hermes was. He glanced across at Jason and smiled, realizing Scott had passed the message on. Ray was able to give their exact position. Three British Sea King Helicopters and two Harrier Jump Jets were immediately launched. It would take less than two minutes for the Harriers to arrive.

"Get ready, the second chopper is coming," Cookie shouted, taking aim with the machine gun. Jack and Ray took aim with the rifles when the boat engine stopped. All eyes looked at Jason who was driving it. He tried starting it, but it failed to respond. The Vietcong helicopter started shooting its machine guns. It came in close. Bullets ricocheted all around the boat and on the deck. Cookie took a bullet to his chest and stopped shooting. The big Scotsman collapsed on the deck floor. Jason climbed out of the wheelhouse and ran to his aid.

He knelt down and placed his hand over the wound. Cookie was losing a lot of blood. The helicopter stopped shooting. It came in really close for a closer inspection. Water spray danced on

Jason's face. He looked up at the helicopter. It was then he saw him, the man next to the pilot with the black patch over his eye; General Chow.

For a brief moment, General Chow and Jason starred at each other. The stare was broken when Ray shot the engine of the helicopter. His second shot hit the pilot's arm. The helicopter spun around smoking while the wounded pilot and General Chow fought to control it. Eventually, it headed straight for the boat. It crashed into the rear, finally coming to rest half on, half off with fuel escaping from the helicopter onto the deck. The rotor blades hit the water and broke up, sending shards of metal in all directions.

Ray was concerned with the leaking fuel and shouted at Jack. "Get Evans off and into the water. This is gonna blow." He made his way to the front of the boat to help Jason. His son was knelt down, trying to prevent more blood loss from Cookie's chest. "We have to get off son, jump."

"I can't leave Cookie," Jason said, fighting back tears. He looked up at his father. His face suddenly changed and he leapt to his feet. He had noticed movement behind his father.

General Chow had climbed out of the helicopter wreckage and onto the boat and glared at Jason.

"You!" The single word was spat out with a mixture of hatred and amusement. Cho straightened himself and aimed his pistol at Ray. Jason acted fact he spun on his right leg and threw a powerful roundhouse kick at his father. His foot caught Ray in the chest and ejected him over the side of the boat. The bullet skimmed past Jason's foot where Ray had been standing.

"Con lai," General Chow said pointing his pistol at Jason.

"Less of the Con lai nonsense. I'm British," Jason shouted. His body was pumped with adrenaline. His muscle fibers contracted like recoiled springs. Once sapphire blue eyes became dilated and turned almost black as he concentrated.

"British boy. You are dead British boy," Chow said in English. It surprised Jason. Cookie forced himself up onto one elbow.

"Jason jump," Cookie shouted.

General chow aimed his pistol and fired two shots at the injured man.

"No!" Jason screamed. He leapt forward and threw himself at General Chow. His fist connected with Chow's gun hand, sending it flying in the air. It was as if Jason stepped outside himself. Seeing Cookie shot twice more broke him. Jason had lost his temper like never before. Using a method Wong Tong had told him only to use in a life and death situation, he pulled back his fist and aligned his body perfectly. His bones and muscles lined up with the target. Jason's fist made a snapping sound before hitting its target. His shoulder followed through with the deadly blow that broke through General Chow's skin, chest muscle, and three ribs. "Keeha,"

Jason shouted.

General Chow's eyes looked up at nothing. His body went into spasms before falling to the deck of the boat. Two of his ribs had splintered and penetrated his heart.

Two of Jason's fingers were dislocated after the forceful blow. His hand became numb. He stood over General Chow, shaking in anger. He had never used the punch before. It would break through two-inch wood and even crack a brick. Wong had always told Jason he must never try it until he was at least eighteen and fully developed. Ray clambered back up onto the boat. He called to Jason and never got a response. Not thinking, Ray caught Jason's arm from behind. Immediately, he was thrown over his shoulder and onto his back. Before he could move Jason had his left hand around his throat and his right fist back ready to strike.

"Jason, it's me," gasped Ray. Jason's eyes were still dilated. His hand trembled over Ray's throat. "Jason it's me, Dad. Get up son, this boat is going to catch fire any second." Ray would never be able to describe the look his son was giving him, but it was terrifying. Something cold and dark. "Snap out of it, Jason."

Jason blinked, took a breath, and released his father. He quickly got his thoughts together. "Cookie," he said. He ran back to the front of the boat. The man was slumped on his front. Jason and Ray rolled him onto his back. He coughed up blood as he tried to speak.

"Don't speak we'll get you help," Jason said in tears. His words where muffled by the roar of the British Harrier Jets hovering above. Cookie mouthed something; Jason leant down and put his ear to his mouth.

"What is it good for?" Cookie croaked through his blood-drenched teeth.

"Absolutely nothing," Jason sniffed back. Cookie's mouth opened a final time as if he tried to smile.

A ball of flames chased across the boat towards them. Ray scooped Jason up and dove into the water. When they came up from under the initial plunge, the whole boat was in flames. The Vietcong boats kept their distant and watched while the Sea King Helicopter rescue team air lift Jack and Evans, followed by Ray and Jason.

Jason said nothing on the short flight back to HMS Hermes. He watched while the crew worked on Evans's wound. The crew gave Ray a warm welcome back to his ship. He offered to have a bed made up in his room for his son. Jason turned the offer down. He preferred to be given no special treatment. He was given a bunk with the naval ratings. He enjoyed being with the regular sailors. They cursed, farted, and talked about girls. It was much more entertaining to a twelve-year-old boy than sleeping in the room with his father.

Chapter Twenty-Eight

Jason was allowed on the ship's bridge the following morning. His father volunteered to resume his duties and the captain agreed. HMS Hermes was given orders to set a course for the United Kingdom.

Jason spoke to Scott via Morse code. Scott had been monitoring the Royal Navy's radio signals. He gave Jason some disturbing news regarding Tay Ninh. Jason immediately asked his father if it was true.

"Dad, Scott said—"

His father interrupted him. "When you are on the bridge and in uniform, you address me as Lieutenant," Ray ordered.

Jason huffed and carried on. "Okay *Lieutenant*, Scott said the village outside of Tay Ninh was burnt and bombed. Is that true?"

Ray got up and flicked through some papers and read them before replying. "It seems so. We never passed through the village. An informer seems to think they helped us escape, so the whole village was wiped out."

Jason's eyes welled up. He marched over to his father and snatched the communication reports and read them.

"Did you go through that village son?" Ray asked. Jason never replied. He was reading everything he could on the reports. Ray asked again and still never got a response.

"The children and Claudette haven't been found. They must be in hiding. We have to help them," Jason said and explained everything to his father.

HMS Hermes sent a coded message to the British admiralty and waited for a response. The ship maintained its position just off the Vietnamese coast and estuary of Ho Ming City waiting for a reply. At seven pm local time, HMS Hermes was given orders to set a course for the UK. Nothing could be done for the villagers outside of Tay Ninh.

Jason slept until almost noon. After he ate, he paced up and down the deck of the Hermes, blaming himself for the possible death of the children. When he noticed the ship start to turn and alter course, he ran up to the bridge and burst in and demanding to know what was happening. The captain was on the bridge talking with his father who was appalled by Jason's behaviour.

"Jason, this is a war ship. You have to act your age you can't just barge in here," Ray snapped

"Why are we moving? What about the orphans at the village?" Jason asked.

"Our orders are to return to the UK. We have done all we can here, son. Get some rest. You still look tired," Ray said. He gently roughed his son's hair.

"I slept for fourteen hours. I'm not tired. I'm worried. We can't just leave them to die." Jason argued.

Ray tried explaining to Jason that unfortunately the children and most of the villagers would have been killed in the bombing and fires. Jason disagreed and stormed out of the bridge.

"Shouldn't you go after him?" The captain asked Ray.

"No, Sir. He's upset with the death of Cookie and I think he blames himself for the village, but he can't exactly go anywhere can he?"

Those words would later haunt Raymond Steed.

*

Three hours later and Seaman Stuart Hill was found unconscious on the lower launch deck. He was carried to sickbay where he explained to his senior officer that Lieutenant Steed's son held him in a headlock and somehow made him pass out.

The captain and Ray briskly marched to the sickbay to hear the story for themselves.

"Are you saying my son Jason knocked you out?" Ray asked.

"Yes, Sir. He moved like lightning. He was putting some fuel cans in an inflatable. I asked what he was doing and he attacked me. Held me in a headlock and was squeezing my neck. Then I remember being asked if I was okay when someone found me, Sir."

"Is your son capable of that, Lieutenant?" the Captain asked.

"Yes, sir. His karate master taught him. They do something to the main artery on the neck."

A voice came from behind. "Sir, an inflatable is missing."

The entire crew on HMS Hermes started an immediate search for Jason, although both the captain and Ray suspected he had left the ship. The British Admiralty were furious with the news and demanded an enquiry into how a twelve-year-boy old could take a motorized inflatable and leave a warship without being seen. They were given new orders to wait in the South China Sea. The whole incident was embarrassing for Raymond Steed.

*

The Royal Marine rigid hull inflatable was perfect for cruising the estuary. Complete with a high-powered outboard engine, it had a rigid fiberglass hull and inflatable rubber tubing around the edges to help with buoyancy. Following a compass, Jason soon picked up the lights of the Ho Chi Minh City river mouth. He had blackened his face and was wearing black clothing. The inflatable was carrying six large cans of fuel. He sailed through the harbor unnoticed. Jason knew he would be in a heap of trouble for running away, stealing an inflatable motorboat, and knocking out an innocent sailor, but deep down he felt he had to do something.

By dawn, Jason was thirty miles up Ong Dong Nai River. He slowed the boat down to a crawl. He was unsure if the Vietcong would still be looking for him now that the British prisoners' escape had become international news. He hoped that they would now forget the matter, especially since General Chow was dead.

"Yes," he said out loud. He found what he had been looking for, the old barge. Making sure his boat was well hidden from passing fishing boats, he tied it next to the barge and set off on foot.

Carrying just a map, compass, and water bottle, he started the arduous journey back into the jungle. He was annoyed with himself for not bringing mosquito repellent. They swooped in and dined on his blood. It was raining again. He plodded forward, heading to the village.

Shick, shick. The sound of a rifle being cocked made him freeze. He slowly turned to his right. Two rifles were pointed at him. A small Vietcong search team looking for survivors of the village were resting. Jason had walked right into them.

He raised his hands and tried his acting dumb routine again, but it didn't work this time.

They had been given his description and were elated to have captured him. Jason was strip-searched and kicked while he was dressing. They took no chances with him. A gun was pointing at him at all times. Jason watched them as they used a radio to contact their superiors. He could tell they were excited with his capture. He was forced to lay face down with his hands on his head while they waited for more troops and a superior officer.

Jason thought he may end up as a prisoner like his father, or his fate may be far worse. They sat around him, laughing and joking every now, and then they poked him with a rifle. He felt humiliated. Worse was yet to come. One of his capturers stood over him and urinated on him. Jason closed his eyes and tried to block out everything they were doing, hoping the nightmare would soon be over.

The stories Jason had heard from the Americans regarding the cruelty they put prisoners through was happening to Jason. The warm urine soaked through his clothing and touched his skin.

He started to get angry and annoyed with himself for not taking more care. He should have crept slowly through the jungle, not marched along like he was out for a Sunday walk. He took his hands from his head and placed them under his chin, trying to keep the mud and urine from his face. He was kicked and shouted at. He ignored them and was kicked again. A guard eventually bent down and pulled Jason's arms back to behind his head again and forced his knee into the back of Jason's head, pushing his face into the mud.

The four soldiers guarding him took a message on the radio. Jason could hear more footsteps. Three soldiers joined the others and stood around Jason. They were ordered to help guard him. The Vietcong high command wanted him alive and would take no chances.

He had made up his mind. He was going to die, and if he was, he would take some with him. The knowledge brought a wave of anger that ignited in Jason's head. His short fuse was awakened. He fought to control his temper. The final straw came when another guard got up and stood over him and started to urinate on him. Jason's entire body started to tremble. His pupils dilated darker than a hundred midnights. If they were trying to provoke him, they had finally succeeded and woken a human hurricane with a sting worse than a Fattail Scorpion.

"Is that *all* the extra men you brought?" he said in a hoarse voice.

What happened next seemed like a blur to the guards. Jason rolled over onto his back and brought his foot up, catching the man in the groin and pulled the guard down on himself. He drew the guard's revolver and shot three shots across at a guard who had a rifle aimed at him. The fourth shot was for the guard on top of him. Jason pushed the body off and leapt to his feet. The three other guards made a grab for their rifles. Jason unloaded the last two bullets in one and swept the feet away of another soldier. As he was falling, Jason took his gun hand and twisted it back, aiming the gun back at the soldier. A single shot in the abdomen made him fall.

The last two guards scrambled for their guns, but Jason threw himself at them.

His right fist smashed into one guard's throat, rupturing his trachea. Jason's right foot demolished the last guards face. He hopped on his left leg, striking the man again and again with his foot. The man's nose and jaw fractured with the unwavering strikes to his face. As he was falling Jason hopped onto his right leg and threw a Mae Geri kick with his left leg sending him flying back several feet.

Jason stood in a fighting stance. His fists clenched, dark dilated eyes darting, looking for anything that moved. He could hear others approaching, swashing through the undergrowth. More Vietcong soldiers where coming. He picked up his water bottle, map, compass, and a rifle. As he fled, he could hear some of his wounded victims moaning and crying for help. He was exhausted. He dug deep inside himself to breathe heavy and move. His pace was slow. He was desperate to rest and catch his breath. His earlier adrenaline rush had sapped all his strength. With gritted teeth, he picked up his pace and started moving faster. He could hear the snapping of branches behind him. He was being pursued.

Chapter Twenty-Nine

After nearly an hour, he eventually stopped running to catch his breath. For once, he welcomed the heavy rain. It washed the mud and his urine stinking clothing. He removed his pants to examine his leg that he had caught on a lower tree branch; it was cut across his thigh and bleeding rapidly. Pulling off his shirtsleeves, he made a bandage. "Don't you ever give up?" he said as he squashed a mosquito that fancied dining on his bare leg.

As he continued on, his pace was slower. His leg burnt with every stride. He had to ignore it and pushed on. The day eventually came to an end. The moonlight, unable to penetrate the thick rain clouds, made it difficult to see ahead.

The clouds cleared and shone a pale blue light across the rainforest. The village was gone, burnt to the ground. It made him feel sick to his stomach that he was the cause of the destruction of the village. The orphanage was just ashes. The slate blackboard that was once supported on a wall lay among the rubble. The chalk writing was still visible.

He took his bearings and set off, hoping that his guess was right and he would find the children.

After going back twice, retracing his steps, he eventually found the entrance to the underground tunnel. Making sure he was not being followed, he lifted the bamboo trap door and climbed down swiftly through the twists and turns in the narrow tunnel.

It was warm and damp like he experienced before but smelt of burning kerosene; the top level was lit up with a burning lamp. He took the steps down to the lower level.

"Jason?" Claudette asked in her strong French accent.

"Well it's not Santa Claus." Jason said in French. The children were relieved to see it was Jason and not the Vietcong. Claudette moved closer to Jason and brushed his long blond fringe away from his eyes and examined his forehead.

"Your hurt! Come here," she said, taking his arm. She sat him down and cleaned a large cut on his forehead. He hadn't noticed it himself and assumed he was sweating, not bleeding. The Vietcong heard we took you in; they destroyed most of the village. It was with God's grace we are still alive and that some of the children knew of this old tunnel."

"No they destroyed *all* the village." Jason sighed. "Can you look at my leg? The cut is deep. A tree branch stabbed me when I was running."

"We thought you had gotten away or had been killed," Claudette said, removing his makeshift bandage on his thigh.

"Ouch, that's painful." He cursed and was given a slap on the back of the hand for cursing. "I came back to help you and you slap me?"

"If I had any soap I would wash out your mouth. Don't use that language in front of the children," Claudette snapped.

"They don't understand French," Jason argued.

"God does. He can hear it."

Jason liked Claudette. She mothered him. He could see why the Amerasian children took to her. When she had finished dressing his wound, he got dressed and looked around and armed himself. He counted twenty-three children. They watched him constantly in bewilderment.

"Can they all walk?" he asked Claudette.

"Yes, but walk where? We are safe here until our food and water runs out."

"You can't stay here. We have to move and get to the South river."

"That's a four hour hike, and it's not going to be easy. Some of these kids are only small. We have a three- and four-year-old." Claudette paused. "If the Vietcong catch us, I dread to think what they may do to the children. They shot some of the villagers."

Jason looked at her wide-eyed. The burning of the village was bad enough. This news made it more painful. "Tell them it's a game or something, but they must be quiet and follow me. We go now. It's dark. We need to make the river before morning."

"No Jason, it's too dangerous."

Jason looked at her and paused while thinking. "You believe God is watching you and has saved you so far. I'm sure your God will look after everyone and keep them all safe."

"Jason he is not my God, he is *our* God. He looks out for you too." Claudette smiled and kissed the cross she was wearing around her neck.

"Well he didn't look out for Cookie." Jason sighed. "Come on, we have to move."

*

Max Fisher was given an audience with President Ford to give him an update. The President was sat at a large table in the Pentagon, signing papers.

"Morning Fisher. What's this I hear that boy stole a boat and went back to 'Nam? Can't the Brits manage to prevent a school boy taking a motor boat?"

"Morning Mr. President, Sir, Yes he got his father and two other British back on the British carrier HMS Hermes and took off," Fisher explained.

"Although he stole a plane from us..." Fisher trailed off wishing he hadn't made the comment.

"Why? He rescued his father. What's his plan now, take on the whole Vietcong army single handed?"

"From what I can gather, Sir, he is a little... shall we say, upset that the Vietcong burnt down a village and an orphanage full of Amerasians. When he heard nothing was being done to help them, he went AWOL," Fisher finished, speaking slowly and softly.

President Ford threw the papers off his desk and stood. He leaned over his desk glaring at Max. "There are no Amerasians. There may be some orphans but they are *not* American and have nothing to do with us. Do I make myself clear?"

"Er, yes, Sir," Fisher stammered.

"Whatever possessed the British to make a person like Jason Steed?" President Ford asked, taking his seat.

"By all accounts, Sir, he is just an ordinary boy. I've met him. He's a normal, cheeky twelve-year-old with vast martial arts knowledge. Add the fact he has faster than average reflexes and was trained to induce a high adrenaline rush into his system, he is a walking lethal weapon. Because of his size and good looks, many under estimate him, and he is able to achieve more. The truth about Jason Steed is that there is not a boy in the world like him," Fisher said.

The president rose from his seat again and wagged his finger. "I'm not sure what he's planning Fisher, but I want to hear no more about Amerasian orphans is that clear?"

"Crystal clear, Mr. President."

*

Jason took the lead. The children snaked behind, following him. Claudette was at the back of the line. The pace was slow. It frustrated Jason. An hour had passed and they hadn't gone very far. He stopped and waited for her to catch up.

Claudette caught up. She had the two youngest boys with her. They held her hand and were both sobbing.

"Shush keep them quiet," Jason snapped. "Why are they crying?"

"They have no shoes and their feet hurt. Don't shush them," Claudette snapped back.

Jason paused and looked at them. He threw away the rifle he was carrying and picked up the four-yearoold and sat him on his shoulders.

"You carry the smaller one, but tell them they must be quiet. We are going on a trip, on a boat to America." Jason sighed.

"What about the rifle?" Claudette asked.

"It won't help. If we get caught, I can't start shooting at the Vietcong. If they shoot back one of the children may get hit. Come on, let's go. Besides, I have some grenades, and I thought you said God would protect us. Let's hope he's watching."

After just a few paces, Jason regretted his bold decision to carry the boy. He was heavier than he expected and it made the going much harder. The journey was agonizingly slow. Torrents of rain cascaded down on them; in some places, the water was waist deep for some of the smaller children. Jason gritted his teeth and pushed on. His neck and shoulder muscles screamed in pain carrying him.

On higher ground, they paused for a rest. Jason was relived to lower the smiling boy down. He held Jason's hand and asked "Phong ve sinh?"

"What did he say?" Jason asked Claudette.

"Phong ve sinh, means he wants to pee. Can you take him behind a tree? I will check the others," Claudette said as a matter of fact. Jason looked down at the little boy who was standing crossed legged.

"Em, what, me take him? Okay but if he needs more than a pee I'm not cleaning him." Jason walked the boy behind some shrubs. "Go on then Phong ve sinh." Jason gestured.

When the boy finished he came back to Jason and held his hand. "That had better be rain water on your hand and nothing else." Jason grinned. The small boy had no idea what his new friend had told him but he felt safe with him.

"Jason, we have to rest. They are tired and

their feet are rubbed raw. Even those with shoes, they are poorly fitting and soaked," she said and passed Jason a water bottle; he shook it.

"It's almost empty," he said unscrewing the cap.

"I had some. That's the last of it. Drink it."

Jason put it to his lips and paused. The small boy he had been carrying watched him.

"What about Tiny Tim here? He hasn't had any." Jason asked.

"He's called An Dung. You need it more than him. You are carrying him; he won't survive unless you make it," Claudette suggested.

"*An Dung?* What kind of name is that! The poor thing. Who is gonna name there kid An Dung?" Jason grinned.

"It means peaceful hero. It's a common name here," Claudette said.

Jason took a mouthful of water and passed the bottle to the small boy. "Here, Tiny Tim. Not much left, but drink it." The boy greedily gulped down the last few drops of water. "And don't worry, I'm not gonna be calling you no *Dung*, Poo, or Manure names. From now on, you are Tiny Tim." Jason smiled as he watched his little friend drink the last of the water.

"We must keep going. We can't spend the day out here tomorrow with no water. I know it's hard, but they must keep up," Jason said picking up, Tiny Tim and lifting him onto his shoulders.

"Very well, but slower, Jason. They are only little and all tired, hungry, and thirsty," Claudette pleaded.

Chapter Thirty

HMS Hermes received a telex message from the British Admiralty. They were to wait another twenty-four hours and, if Jason had not returned by then, they where to set its course for the UK. Ray was beside himself with worry; no one had heard anything from Vietnam. Doubts started to spread among the crew regarding Jason survival.

Max Fisher and his intelligence sources reached out to contacts in Vietnam. No one had any information on his whereabouts; nothing had been seen of him or the children. Some started to even doubt that there was an orphanage full of Amerasian children. The Ford administration at the White House wanted to keep it that way. The US media was still running with stories of atrocities carried out by US troops to local woman and children. The last thing they wanted was a truckload of Amerasian kids turning up on the ten o'clock news.

*

Jason, Claudette, and the children trundled through the jungle. They stopped and hushed the children. They could here shouting coming from behind. Jason lowered Tiny Tim down and clambered up a tree for a better view.

He quickly scuffled back down. “The Vietcong are right behind us. Keep going. I will catch up,” Jason told Claudette.

He tied some twines across the path and wedged a grenade between a tree root. Carefully, he tied the twine to the grenade pin. He placed the others next to it and covered them with leaves. The Vietcong where gaining and would have him in their sights at any moment. Once his trap was set, he ran and caught up with Claudette. He swooped Tiny Tim up in his arms.

“Claudette, we must hurry now. They are right behind us. Hopefully, there will be a big bang.” Jason panted.

He pushed forward with the boy in his arms. A minute later and a huge explosion erupted behind them. The children screamed. Jason kept moving forward. Claudette and the children followed. A huge fist of black smoke escaped from the explosion that threatened to smack the clouds.

After twenty minutes, Jason stopped and took Tiny Tim off his shoulders. His shoulders and neck were stiff. He rotated his arms to bring them back to life. Claudette caught up with him.

“Jason, we have to stop. I can’t walk another step.” She lowered the boy down that she was carrying. The other children sat around on the floor. they all looked in discomfort.

"We made it. Here's the barge." He smiled and started pulling off branches and large palm leaves.

"This, does it have an engine?" she asked.

"No, but that does. I will tow it," Jason said pointing at the Navy rigid hull inflatable. "It's got plenty of fuel and a huge engine. I think it will pull it okay."

Claudette reluctantly agreed but had her doubts. Once he had cleared the debris, he had Claudette get all the children on board the barge, except Tiny Tim who stuck close to Jason's side and refused to leave. They tied the front of the barge to the navy raft. Tiny Tim was put in a lifejacket so big his head just popped out the top.

"You look like a turtle now." Jason grinned. The small boy smiled, revealing a perfect set of baby white teeth.

Jason pulled the rope on the starter. The engine roared into life. Slowly, he pulled off. The barge held fast and refused to budge. The children watched the outboard motor churn the water and waited for it to move. "Jason, it's not working. Your boat is too small to pull us," Claudette shouted over the engine noise.

"Come on, move," Jason said under his breath. He opened the throttle to full power the rope strained nothing happen. "It's stuck." Jason pulled back on the rope and jumped into the water and waded around the barge, trying to push it.

Two of the children started pointing at something in the jungle and looked terrified. “Jason they have seen soldiers. We have to surrender,” Claudette screamed. Her normal calm, easy nature had disappeared. Jason noticed the panic in her face. He looked back at the jungle. Some three hundred feet away three Vietcong were running towards them.

“Rock it,” Jason shouted.

“Language, Jason,” Claudette scorned, thinking he said something else.

“No rock the barge, from side to side like this,” Jason said, leaping onto the barge. “Rock it, rock it.” He shouted to her and the children. The barge responded and rocked from side to side. He leapt into the water and waded back to the inflatable. He smiled when he noticed Tiny Tim was unnecessarily rocking that as well.

He opened the throttle up. Smoke and water spray covered the barge. The Vietcong soldiers ran towards the barge. It moved a foot. The more the children rocked it from side to side, it slowly moved from the ground and was getting into deeper water. One solider caught hold of the barge and started shouting at the children. Jason held Tiny Tim’s hands on the throttle. “Hold it here okay?” he said to the boy.

Jason leapt into the water and waded back to the barge and headed for the soldier. He caught the soldier’s wrist and twisted it back. “Let go idiot.” Jason cursed. The soldier tried fighting back. He was kneed in the groin. As he crumpled, Jason took his revolver and fired two warning shots at the other two soldiers who were fast approaching.

"Jason," Claudette screamed. The barge was finally free and heading out into the river, being pulled by the inflatable. Tiny Tim was still holding the throttle as Jason showed him. Jason dived into the water and swam as fast as he could towards the barge. He managed to grip the side and pulled himself up. He ran across the barge and caught the rope. He pulled it shorter, pulling it closer to the inflatable. When it was close enough, he leapt onto the inflatable.

"Good job," Jason said, taking the controls. The barge followed behind and into deep water. Eventually, he slowed down and headed downriver, constantly looking back, concerned that they would be followed. He was expecting to see a Vietcong motor launch at any moment.

Claudette and the other children were singing on the barge. They seemed happy, unaware of the dangers that lurked around every bend in the river. Jason briefly turned the engine off to refuel and carried on. Tiny Tim fell asleep. A strange feeling came across Jason; it was quiet as they passed Ho Chi Minh City. They were left alone. Fishing canoes and boats kept a safe distance. A Vietcong motor launch patrolled along the river's edge but ignored Jason's inflatable towing the old barge.

Six North Vietnamese River Patrol boats and a Russian built Petya torpedo-carrying Frigate with four-twin machine gun turrets cruised outside the mouth of the river estuary. on red alert and waiting for orders from high command.

*

The crew on the bridge of HMS Hermes watched as the United States Navy ship, USS Dubuque, made a slow pass by. The five hundred and seventy foot ship was two hundred shorter than the Hermes. As well as carrying helicopters, it also carried highly powered small watercraft and amphibious vehicles.

"What's she doing here?" the captain said out loud.

"Not sure. I thought the Yanks had pulled out completely, Sir." Raymond Steed said.

The USS Dubuque slowed down to a crawl just outside the mouth of the river in the South China Sea.

*

Jason could see the sea the water was getting choppy and bounced the inflatable raft around as it pulled the heavy barge. His heart sank as from both sides of the river mouth came four Vietcong armored motor launches. He had no radio, just a revolver with a couple of bullets left. Out of any option, his only choice was to try and make a run for it. On full throttle, the water splashed up on the barge once more.

Claudette and the children looked up, wondering why he was going faster. They didn't have to ask they could see the approaching vessels. Claudette shouted something to Jason. He nodded, even though he couldn't hear what she said.

*

"Sir, there's something on the radar. Something's happening," the HMS Hermes' radar operator reported. The captain and Lieutenant Steed looked for themselves. "Look, Sir. Four boats from each side rapidly approaching the smaller craft in the center that is heading out towards us."

"Steed, do you think that's your boy?" the captain asked, sucking on his pipe and peering at the screen.

"I don't know, but who else would they be chasing. Can we help him, Sir?"

"The Yanks are closer and have started moving again towards him."

The radio operator became excited again. "Sir, the Vietnamese Petya Frigate is also on the move."

*

Jason noticed the USS Dubuque. He was unsure what country it was to start with, fearing it was Vietnamese until he could pick out the Stars and Stripes flying proudly. The Vietcong fired a round of warning shots, one hitting the barge. Jason slowed down to a crawl. If he was on his own, he would have made a run for it. But with so many lives at stake, he had to obey.

The Vietcong approached and told him to stop. He ignored them and kept it slowly moving closer to the USS Dubuque. Two rifles were pointed at Jason. Claudette shouted at them. “He is just a boy. These are refugees, just children.”

For a few tense moments nothing was done. The Vietcong seemed unsure what to do. They didn’t have orders to shoot children and the USS Dubuque was getting closer. The Vietcong fired another warning shot, this time at Jason’s raft.

“Claudette, tell them to stop. I have Tiny Tim here,” He shouted in French and lifted Tim in his arms. She shouted back at them and argued again that they were refugees and meant no one any harm.

The USS Dubuque sent an armored motor launch. They had strict instructions not to open fire on the Vietcong, even if they were fired at. Jason smiled when he saw them approaching. “These are Amerasian refugees, they need water and food thanks for helping,” Jason shouted at the American launch.

“No, son, we are not able to take refuges. We advise you to turn back to Vietnam with them,” an American voice said over a speaker.

“What, are you bloody crazy? They will get killed and so will Claudette. She is French. You have to help,” Jason shouted back.

The Americans pulled up closer to Jason's inflatable. He watched as an officer made his way to the side. To his horror, two American soldiers had rifles pointed at Jason.

Jason thought the officer looked around thirty. He was moderately handsome, but sharply angled eyebrows and slicked back hair gave him a vampirish quality. "You must be Jason Steed?"

"Yes, Sir. If you know that, why are your crew pointing guns at me?"

"Your orders are to return the children back where they belong, to Vietnam. That order comes from the highest authority."

"You're having a laugh. First of all if I do, they will kill them, and me, and probably Claudette. No. And Claudette has it from a higher authority. She says God is watching over us, so I guess that trumps your guy. Beside these are Amerasian children. They're half American," Jason argued.

"My orders are to ensure they stay in Vietnam. I have to advise you to turn back."

Jason studied his surroundings. He was surrounded by Vietcong armed motor launches. The US armoured patrol boat and in the shadow of the USS Dubuque. He felt uneasy having so many guns pointed at him from different directions and from both sides. "What would Wong Tong do?" he said to Tiny Tim. "That's right, the opposite to what they expect."

"I like you Americans. I love your country and your root beer and chocolate malt drink are awesome, but I'm British and we never, never *ever* give up. These are half *American* children, and I'm a student at Quentin Roosevelt Military Academy. I'm sure your orders were to send us back for some crazy political reason, but I bet no one gave you an order to shoot children."

"You want to bet on that?" the officer asked.

Jason opened the throttle of the inflatable and pulled away from the Americans. The Vietcong were unsure what to do. The Americans were just as bewildered. They got back on the radio and requested advice. Their orders were again to prevent Jason and the children leaving, but without deadly force. Two shots were fired at Jason's inflatable; they both hit the outboard motor and stopped it.

Chapter Thirty-One

Using the secret codes Jason had sent to his best friend, Scott Turner had been able to monitor all the radio messages and passed them on to the British Admiralty. He also made some calls to several news agencies around the world regarding the rescue of the orphans.

*

An ear blasting ships foghorn was sounded. The HMS Hermes approached and cast a huge shadow over all the boats. The Vietcong vessels dispersed. The Americans kept back as it launched two jump jets and six inflatable crafts

The US officer's launch approached again. "Jason, you don't want to do this. You will be up setting some people in very high places. I have given you the order to return."

"You will have to say you got here too late and never told me to go back. That way, neither of us get into trouble." Jason grinned.

"And why would I do that? I am not in trouble," the officer asked.

"Well this inflatable is a British Naval Raft and you don't want the British government to ask your government why you shot at it with two children on board, do you? Especially when the newspaper people find out how I rescued all these children. Or we could say you helped save them." Jason smiled.

The officer replied but his voice was drowned out by the noise of the Harrier jets and motor crafts.

Two news team helicopters approached and started filming. The children were taken off the barge and transferred to the inflatable's and then onto HMS Hermes. One of the inflatable's towed Jason and Tiny Tim's raft back. Jason noticed his father and Captain Bass watching as some of the crew helped the children aboard. They noticed Jason's raft being towed to the ship rear boat dock and approached.

"Hi Dad, er I mean Lieutenant. Hi Captain, Sir. Um I brought the inflatable back in one piece, but the engine was shot by the Yanks and the Vietcong shot a hole in the side. It's loosing air, but I'm sure we can patch her up," Jason stuttered. "This is Tiny Tim. His real name is An Dung or something but I think he likes Tim, um. Am I in much trouble?" Both men couldn't help smiling at his cheeky grin.

"I'm glad you're safe, son. Your father has been worried. You keep doing that and his hair will be as grey as mine." Captain Bass scoffed. Ray helped Tiny Tim onto the Hermes loading dock and held out his hand for Jason. In a swift move he pulled Jason from the inflatable into his arms.

"Don't keep doing this to me, son. I'm not superhuman. I can't stand this. Have you any idea how worried I have been?" Ray said. He noticed the small boy was also hugging Jason. "Who's this little chap?"

"Dad, this is Tiny Tim. Can we keep him?" Jason said roughing the small boy's hair.

"No, Jason. He's not a dog. The American authorities will want to find him a suitable home for him with a family."

"We're a family and the Americans didn't want them." Jason smiled.

"No, I'm at sea most of the time and you," he paused. "Well *you,* sonny boy, are where ever you want to be."

United States President Ford made a speech to the world's media. He told them how. in a joint American and English operation, some refugees from Vietnam had been rescued. When asked by a reporter regarding the children's heritage being Amerasian, he failed to answer the question and talked about how America prides itself on being a melting pot for all races and religions, and the children were very welcome.

*

Jason's problems continued. Quentin Roosevelt Military Academy refused to allow him back after he went absent without leave. The British government put pressure on the Americans to keep Jason's identity a secret. The Americans argued it was an American military academy student who broke the prisoners free. The British argued if his identity was published it may prevent SYUI from using him again. They could see the promising career he had as an agent.

Raymond told Jason that he needed to get back to his studies and forget about being an agent for a few years. Jason was devastated to hear that he would have to go back to St. Joseph's, a school he hated.

After ten days, HMS Hermes reached the Royal Australian Naval Base in Fremantle. The children were taken into care where they would be eventually flown to the United States. Jason was upset saying goodbye to Tiny Tim. He grew fond of the smaller boy, as if he was a little brother.

The surviving prisoners spoke at a press conference in Freemantle. It was heart wrenching for the relatives of those that never survived. Ray spoke and gracefully said that they would never have gotten away without the help of Marcel and the others. No mention was given regarding Jason. He watched from the back of the room, his hand still bandaged. A large photographer pushed Jason out of the way so he could get a better picture of Ray, Evans, and Jones.

On the car ride back to the HMS Hermes, Jason was quiet. He forced a smile and told his father he agreed with SYUI and the British government to be kept away from the limelight. Secretly, he was hurt. In a phone conversation with Scott two hours later he told Scott. “Now, I know how the horse feels like when the jockey gets all the praise for winning a horse race.”

He was granted permission to stay on board HMS Hermes for another five weeks while it cruised back to the UK, although it was no holiday. He was given duties to do as any sailor or able seaman would.

The return of HMS Hermes at Plymouth was a minor occasion in the UK. A few welcome home banners like any returning naval ship. Jason and his father had not made a decision on what school he would return to after the summer recess. The answer came quicker than they expected. An overweight man stood smoking a cigarette on the loading dock, waiting for Jason.

“George.” Jason grinned. He ran forward and gave George a hug. “Thanks for coming to welcome us back.”

“Really, George, you couldn’t wait for him to get home before you need to steal him away?” Ray cursed.

“Okay I admit it, I did need to ask if he could help out in a delicate situation that is very close to home to you guys, but I also wanted to welcome you *both* back. I’m pleased you’re safe Ray. I know you and I don't always see eye to eye." George said offering his hand.

Ray shook his hand and grunted back. "What's this delicate situation that's also close to home?"

"Let's get a cup of tea shall we?"

*

Ray and George sat at a table with a mug of tea in a local café. Jason put some money in the jukebox and chose some records.

"Okay, you got my attention. But before you start, you know he's not going to go on a mission again," Ray said.

Jason sat down next to his father and slurped a milk shake through a straw. "Agh, this is crap compared to what I had in America. Those malt shakes are awesome," Jason said pulling a face.

"It's what?" Ray sternly asked.

"Oh, um sorry, Dad. I meant it's nasty," Jason said.

"Just because you spent a few weeks with a bunch of sailors doesn't mean you use that language in front of me," Ray said before turning his scornful look at George. "Look, George. You know I won't agree to Jason helping you on a mission. He has just missed a ton of school work, and I will not put him in danger."

"I'm fine, Dad. I can look after myself," Jason argued.

"No, you're not. I have not forgotten how you got on the boat when Cookie got shot. You completely lost it and..." He paused and took a sip of his tea. "No, Jason. Enjoy the summer recess with Scott, meet up with Catherine, and we will discuss where you go after recess later. But no missions."

George looked at Jason. "Before I start, Max Fisher in America wanted me to thank you for them, Jason. Apparently your tip on a Corporal Jones was right. He was an undercover spy and was working for the Chinese intelligence agency. The Yanks have arrested him. Although Max also called you a disobedient little monkey, but he used much stronger language of course," George said with a smile.

George pulled a brown file out of his briefcase. The outside was stamped in red letters TOP SECRET. The wordings immediately caught Jason's attention. "I know Ray, after all, I agreed not to send him on any missions. Well, apart from helping you out when Bill Giles' niece went missing, and Jason soon solved that. But, I think you will find this is very close to home."

He opened the file and pulled out a large black and white photograph and slid the picture across the table. It was of a man in his early forties, wearing a duffle coat and smoking a cigarette. Jason looked at the picture briefly before Ray pushed it back across the table.

"Not very close to home George I don't know him," Ray said.

"And I should hope bloody not. This is Shamus O'Neill. He is a suspected member of the Irish Republican Army and their number one arms dealer."

"What of it? I'm sure there are many like him," Ray scoffed.

"Yes, you're right, but we believe Shamus is responsible for many of the bombings. He's an explosive expert and has been active for the IRA for fifteen years," George said.

"Arrest him then," Jason said.

"We have no proof. I do know that he and his wife have been trying to have a child for years and have finally given up, so they just completed an application with Belfast City Council to be foster parents," George said.

Ray laughed. "You are pathetic, George. No way would I agree to sending Jason in as a foster child. Come on, Jason, we have a long drive home." Ray got up from his seat and nudged Jason out. They started walking towards the door and Jason stopped in his tracks.

"George, why did you say this mission was *close to home*? You made it sound like we knew him." Jason asked.

"We believe he planted a certain bomb in

1962. It was meant for the defence secretary and his wife, but it was planted on a similar black Rover outside the same theatre. It killed the occupants, a Mr. and Mrs. Steed. Your parents, Ray."

Ray marched back and picked up the picture. "This piece of dirt was responsible?"

"Everything leads to him. He has planted many more since and killed dozens more and maimed countless others," George said.

"He's the guy who killed my grandparents before I was born dad?" Jason asked.

"Yes, I actually met your mother at the airport after the funeral,. I literally bumped into her."

"Then this time it's personal," Jason said taking the picture from his father.

"No, Jason. You're not doing it. Plus I need you to talk to someone about your problem. It's got worse now you're getting older," his father said.

"What problem?" Jason said, frowning at his father.

"Your temper. After you finished off General Chow, you were pretty much out of it. You had me pinned down by my throat and were going to hit me," Ray said.

Jason sighed and sat back down. He looked at his father and George. "The adrenaline rush I induce into my system makes me alert and defensive. If I get hurt or lose my temper in a fight it kind of gets out of control. Maybe I should go to Hong Kong for a few weeks and spend time with Wong Tong for extra training, em, I mean help with it."

"Sounds like a bloody good plan," George said to Ray. "Send him to Hong Kong for a few weeks to train with his karate master. Then maybe we can look at catching your parents killers."

Chapter Thirty-Two

Jason returned to Hong Kong for three weeks to work with his karate master Wong Tong. As far as Ray was concerned, he was getting help with his temper. Jason, however, used it as an opportunity to work with Wong Tong every day, training and improving his martial art skills.

Jason stayed at Wong Tong's modest apartment above the karate studio. The thin, grey haired old man treated Jason like a son. Jason marvelled listening to him, watching his every move, how he twirled his long moustache that hung below his chin.

Wong Tong tried to get Jason to wear traditional Chinese clothing. He tried it once but thought he looked like a girl so removed it, preferring to wear his western clothing.

Before sunrise every morning, Wong Tong and Jason would climb what was locally called 'the Peak' in Hong Kong. Wong Tong would meditate for an hour while the sun rose. Jason would sit with his back against a rock quietly thinking, allowing the sunlight to slowly warm his face. At almost two thousand feet above sea level it was the highest point in Hong Kong.

The clean air filled his lungs. The over populated buildings were hidden from him. He might be the only person in the world, looking at a scene that has remained unchanged for hundreds of years. From his vantage point he could see the vast range of mountains and to the north, the South China Sea. The troubles in Vietnam or the rest of the world meant nothing up here.

It took Jason a while to get over Vietnam. The scars and bruises soon healed on his fit young body. It was the deeper emotional scars that would take time to heal. Making friends with boys at the American military academy and with Cookie one moment, and the next knowing he would never see them again was tough to bear. Jason consoled himself again. No matter what happened in life, when it really came down to it, there was only one person he could really rely on and one person who he could always count on. That person was called Jason Steed.

Book 4 Jason Steed Wolf's Lair.

Find out what happens to Jason in Hong Kong and if he is allowed to take on the mission that will prove to be his most difficult—to become part of the family of the very man that murdered his own grandparents. Book 4, is Jason's toughest assignment yet. He is forced to make one of the most difficult decisions of his life that could have fatal consequences for someone that he is very close too

Book 1 Fledgling Jason Steed

Book 2 Jason Steed Revenge

Book 3 Jason Steed Absolutely Nothing

Book 4 Jason Steed Wolf's Lair

Other books by the author.

Edelweiss Pirates *Operation Einstein.*

Mark A. Cooper

Set during World War Two.

A group of fun loving rebellious German teens calling themselves the Edelweiss Pirates, witness something so deplorably sickening they decide to take action when a six-year old Jewish girl is left orphaned. Torn between patriotism for the country they love and there own rights and freedoms they have to try and do the unthinkable, but with the Gestapo and Hitler Youth hot on their trail, is it too late?

www.markacooper.com

Made in the USA
Charleston, SC
24 April 2015